To J

Clover House
By

Alan Cuthbertson

Clover House

This book is dedicated to

Lily Cuthbertson

and

to the original Julie Sykes

Also a special thanks to Heather

for all her patience and support

Along with Stacey Cuthbertson,

Ashlie Walker, Sue Donkin

and Ruth Draisey.

Book cover design: Craig Cooper

Contact Alan Cuthbertson at
www.alancuthbertson.com

Clover House
Clover House
Chapter 1

Clover House was built in 1770 by the famous mill owner, Benjamin Gott, as a wedding gift for his son William. This large, imposing edifice, situated on the outskirts of Leeds had been vacant for nearly 30 years. That was until the Local Council purchased it and converted it into a home used by the Social Services back in the 1990s. The 'residents', as they are referred to, come from all walks of life, but all have one thing in common: they either have no family or none that can cope with their behavioural problems.

The person responsible for the day-to-day running of the home is Mark Jacobs. He has held the position since it's opening. Alas his hopes and aspirations for Clover House, as being the flag ship of Leeds City Council's Social Services Department, receded over the years along with his hair line. The budget cuts and pressures from on high have taken their toll, both on his enthusiasm and the building itself. He now finds himself struggling to keep his head above water, as rarely are any of the twelve beds vacant and rarely are all the staff positions full.

Inside the building, not much of the infrastructure has changed. Of course it had been rewired, plumbed and decorated, but that was some

Clover House

years ago now and the age of the building is beginning to rear its ugly head here and there. Damp was a problem and the radiators rumbled during the night. There must also be a problem with the electrics to the hall light as the bulb needs changing every two weeks. Jacobs continued to fill in request forms, but replies referring to hard times and budget cuts were the inevitable reply.

The majority of the 8 bedrooms were designed for sharing, fortunately the size of each allowed for this, but the rule was never more than two to a room and strictly no sharing by the opposite sex. Mark Jacobs and the rest of the staff knew that some 'bed hopping' was inevitable, but as there were only two members of staff on the premises during the night, other than sleeping on the landing or locking all the doors, there was little they could do about it. For entertainment there was a TV room and two computers. These were often the cause of many of the home's arguments as the 'residents', especially the males, would literally fight over the consoles and remote controls.

Most of the people housed at the home considered their time there as a sentence, and like most prisoners needed something to stop the boredom. One such 'resident', Leo French, was about to get just that.

Clover House
Chapter 2

Leo was of West African descent. He was skinny and about 5 feet 8 inches tall. He had a limp but nobody really knew why or even bothered to ask how it had come about, and they weren't even sure if Leo knew. He tended to keep himself to himself. He had learnt that if you made friends with anybody they either left the home or just 'shit on you in another way'. He was happy with his own company. He'd been at Clover House longer than any of the other 'residents'. In fact he doesn't even remember much of his early life. He vaguely remembers being told that his mother could no longer handle his behaviour, though all he can recall about her is the smell of cigarettes and whisky. With regards his father he remembers nothing. He left home with another woman while he was still in his mother's stomach and hadn't been mentioned since.

He wandered through into the lounge and found that the television still hadn't been replaced. Last week Tommy Bishop had kicked it over when he got a question wrong whilst watching a game show. Mr Jacobs went ballistic, but in fairness it must have been fifteen years old and due for renewal.

He changed direction and headed towards the computers. Johnny Fish was playing on one so he positioned the seat next to him. As if by magic, as he

Clover House

lowered himself into the chair, it disappeared. He lay there on the floor looking up Tommy Bishop towered over him, his chair in his right hand.

"My chair I believe, hahaha" said Bishop with globules of spit flying out of his mouth as he laughed. Leo rolled away, stood up and rubbed his behind. What Bishop didn't see was as Leo rolled away he pulled the plug from the wall for the computer he was about to use. As he left the room, he smiled, looking over his shoulder he found Bishop thumping the keyboard and smacking the side of the display screen. His curses would make a Liverpool Docker blush.

It was a Saturday so most of the residents were in today, milling around doing their chores. Leo wasn't sure it was legal to make the residents actually do work in the home but to be honest he didn't mind helping here and there. Setting the table was one of his jobs and, as it was coming up to lunch time, he thought he might as well make a start. The cook was called Marge. A chesty woman with a foreign accent and a nasty habit of picking her nose when she thought no one was looking. She was pleasant enough and always ended her greetings to Leo with "...and how is your day?" A question he never knew how to answer, especially when setting the breakfast table, as it hadn't started yet.

Clover House

He wasn't sure where she was from and thought it maybe impolite to ask, so in his over active imagination he pictured her as a refugee from some war struck country, checking the post every day for news of her husband who's fighting some unwinnable war on some miserable Continent. The sad thing is, the way the world is today that could well be the truth.

"What's for lunch today, Marge? He said knowing the answer.

"Bangers and mash" she said, pointing a long knife at him. "And vell you know, seeing as ve have had it every Saturday since I have been vorking here... and that must be ten years."

"You've been working here since you were fourteen?" asked Leo with a mischievous grin. Marge shook her head side to side. "That silver tongue vill get you in trouble one of these days. Now go and tell the others it is almost ready."

All the seats around the long oak table were full, except that is the one next to Leo's. The vacancy was due to his best friend Si (short for Simon) leaving the home two days earlier. There had been no explanation. He just wasn't there one morning. The dining room was alive with chatter and Leo was on his feet helping to serve lunch. As usual everybody

Clover House

either complained about the amount they were given or the quality of the food.

Suddenly the dining room door slid open and in walked Mark Jacobs with what they all presumed was Si's replacement. As always when a new resident arrives, people stop what they are doing and eye the newcomer with a combination of curiosity and suspicion. In such a small environment new additions were kept at arm's length until they had earned their place. Trust was a rare commodity at Clover House.

"This is Julie Sykes." Jacobs announced. "She's going to be staying with us and I'm sure you'll all give her the Clover House welcome." Begrudgingly they put down their knives and forks and began to applaud. Unfortunately instead of a warm welcome, as it was intended to be when the tradition was introduced, it turned in to a slow hand clap that made the room feel more intimidating. This continued for about thirty seconds before an annoyed Mark Jacobs raised his hands to stop the noise. "Just put your case in the corner over there Julie. Have something to eat and you will be shown your room later. Leo will you show Julie around after lunch, introduce her to people, show her what's what, etc?"

"Sure Mister Jacobs," said Leo and nodded for her to take the empty seat next to his. He hated this job. Just because he'd been here the longest he was

Clover House

always given the task of showing newcomers around. The problem was that once he'd finished he inevitably couldn't get rid of them. They would follow him around like a wounded dog.

The meal finished without any other distractions and everybody sloped off leaving Marge and Leo to clear the table and load the dishwasher.

"I'll finish this Leo. You go and entertain your new friend." Marge said this with a whisper and a sly wink. Leo tutted and left the room knowing that his new companion would follow automatically.

In the lounge he sat purposely on one of the large comfy chairs. If he'd sat on the sofa there was every chance she would have sat very close to him and he didn't want people getting the wrong idea. Instead she stood right in front of him waiting like a dog for his next order, or his master to throw something to be retrieved. Leo eyed her up and down as if seeing her for the first time. Her hair was cut quite short and had the faintest hint of blue dye masking its true colour. Her earrings didn't match. One was a stud the other a single hanging pearl. Her t-shirt advertised the band 'Living Zombies', whoever they were. Her skirt was a little too short (in his opinion) and her trainers looked like they needed replacing. All things considered she gave off the 'vibe' of a walking anarchist or someone who seriously needed to buy a mirror.

Clover House

"I didn't ask to be put with you," she stated putting one hand on a hip that was slightly thrust out. "I can find my own way around." Her top lip was raised slightly on the left, the face all teenage girls seem to pull when wanting to look defiant.

Leo smirked. "Well that makes us even, cos I didn't ask for you either." Julie pivoted on one foot and started for the door. "Just a minute," shouted Leo. A newcomer with attitude, this was a first he thought. He nodded to the vacant seat opposite him. "Sit down; I'll give you the low down on this place." Julie turned and thought for a second. Eventually she sidled across the room and sat down, legs crossed and arms folded.

"Okay firstly, who's who." Leo turned his head 180 degrees one way and then the other. In a whisper and leaning forward so Julie could hear, he said, "the big fat guy on the computer, that's Tommy. Keep out of his way. He's a bully and a nutter. The smaller guy sat next to him on the other computer, that's Fish or Johnny Fish to you. He's okay but doesn't talk much. He shares a bedroom with Tommy." On the floor near their feet someone sat building Lego bricks, getting frustrated when they fell over. "This is Wee Willy." Leo pointed with his foot.

"He's called, Wee Willy? Is he Scottish?" asked Julie, smiling at the little frustrated builder.

Clover House

Leo let out a chuckle. "No. We call him that cos he doesn't always make it to the toilet. He's not expected to be here long, just while his mother is in hospital, a few weeks or so."

"Who's she?" asked Julie pointing discretely at a portly female munching on a packet of crisps.

"That's Fat Mary." Leo replied.

Julie was taken back. "That's not very nice," she said disapprovingly.

"Get used to it. In here people tend to call it as they see it. Wait till they give you your name," Leo said smiling and looking her up and down again, trying to imagine what unkind label she will inherit.

"The two over there," Julie turned to see two identical twins playing cards with each other. Not only were they identical in every way but they were both wearing the same clothes. If you had put a sheet of glass between them you would have thought that it was a mirror. Leo continued, "They're called Christopher and Stewart. Don't bother remembering the names because they only ever talk to each other." Then Leo corrected himself, "Actually you can talk to them, but they won't reply."

"There are another couple of males, I use that term loosely, and you'll know why when you see them. James and Dave, but they are out at the moment."

Clover House

A tall, lean man about 30 years old walked in to the room. He nodded in Leo's direction and said, "How's it going Leo?" Leo sat to attention then changed his mind. He stood up to address the man who was wearing overalls and a Leeds United cap.

"Fine, Mister Green. Any idea when the new TV is coming?"

"It should be here this afternoon, Leo. But don't go expecting one of those new fancy 'smart' things." Leo smiled back. He'd been here long enough to keep his expectations low when it came to things happening at Clover House.

"Looking forward to the trip tomorrow Leo?" asked Mr Green.

"Can't wait," replied Leo with more than a hint of sarcasm in his voice.

"That's Mister Green," Leo said to Julie as he sat back down again.

"I gathered that." Again, she was wearing that teenage face. "What trip is he talking about?"

"We are all going to the Urban Farm. He's okay is Mr Green, he's like the handyman around here as well as helping out in general, especially when it kicks-off." Leo added this last bit nonchalantly.

Julie frowned, looked about her then asked, "What do you mean 'kicks-off'?"

Clover House

Leo struggled for the right words but decided not to flower it. "Sometimes it gets a little heated around here and it...'kicks-off'."

"You mean violence?" Julie's expression turned to one of deep concern.

"Not often. You have to realise some people are in here because they can't control their temper. If you see a situation, and you will get to recognise them, a situation that looks like it's getting out of control or turning nasty, just go to your room."

Julie's eyes flicked side to side like a ventriloquist dummy. "Don't worry about it. It doesn't happen often. I just thought you had better be aware that it can." Leo realised he'd scared the newcomer and felt a little guilty. He tried to lighten the situation, "Fancy coming down to the arcade?" He punctuated this with a smile.

Julie considered her options then said, "Okay but I have to take my bag to my room first, I don't want anything being nicked if this place is as bad as you say."

Leo rose slowly from the chair. His bad leg was giving him a few twinges today, probably made worse by Tommy pulling away his chair earlier. "I'll ask Mister Jacobs what room you're in."

"Bedroom 2. He told me when I first arrived," Julie said as she made her way towards her waiting bag in the corner of the dining room.

Clover House

"You are in bedroom 2? But that's a single. Nobody gets a room to themselves when they first arrive. What's so special about you that you haven't told me Julie Sykes?"

Julie looked a little embarrassed by the question. She picked up her bag and scurried towards the staircase without offering a reply. Leo watched her climb the stairs and decided to await her return in the TV lounge.

Julie returned to find Leo in deep conversation with a tall slim woman wearing a white uniform, similar to that worn by a nurse or maybe someone who works in a nail parlour. She waited by the door not wanting to interrupt. Eventually Leo noticed her and said something that brought the exchange to a close. Julie's name must have been mentioned because the woman looked in her direction then back to Leo. She smiled, stroked the side of Leo's arm, winked at him and walked away.

Leo approached Julie, "Ready to go?"

"Who was that?" she asked watching the woman start a new conversation with Mr Green.

"That's Miss Stevenson," he replied as if the answer was obvious. "She's...," he paused looking for the right words. "...she's a kind of nurse. She calls in everyday making sure everyone is okay and handing out medication to those that need it."

Clover House

"She stroked your arm and winked at you." Leo wasn't sure if this was a question, a statement or an observation.

"What can I say? You either have it or you don't." A cheeky grin spread across his face.

Julie looked confused. "Not only is it inappropriate, there must be at least twenty years difference between you."

"Like I said, what can I say? Come on are we going to the arcade or not, I need to get out of here." Leo walked to the front door and picked out his trainers from the long line of assorted footwear against the wall. He slid them on without undoing the laces, opened the door and stepped outside. Julie followed him and closed the large heavy door behind her.

Outside on the wall next to the door was a brass plaque that said CLOVER HOUSE. "Why did they call it Clover House?" asked Julie sliding her forefinger over the letters.

"If you ask any of the staff they won't be able to answer that." Leo said this with a knowing, cocky expression.

"But you can?" asked Julie with raised eyebrows. "Pray tell."

Leo smiled and without breaking eye contact he said "checkout the lawn." Julie looked over his

Clover House

shoulder at the small lawn that grew either side of the gravel path.

She wasn't really sure what she was looking at. "What?" she asked.

"Look closer," said Leo stepping out of the way so she could walk on to the grass. Julie took a couple of steps bent her head slightly and looked closer.

"How imaginative, naming a house after a few weeds you can't get rid of."

Leo smiled. "Look closer." She looked back at the clover scattered about the lawn. To get a closer look she knelt down, regretting it immediately as the grass was still damp from the previous days rain.

She looked back at Leo. "What the hell am I supposed to be seeing?"

Leo smiled. "Pick one." Julie looked back at the clover, picked one and looked back at Leo suspecting she was the victim of some kind of joke. "Now look closer," he added.

"Oh my God," said Julie staring at the four perfectly formed leaves. "It has four leaves; these are supposed to be rare."

Leo just stood watching her. He'd never shared his discovery with anyone else. "Pick another one." Julie selected another at random and held it up to the light.

"Another four leave clover!" she said.

Clover House

"They all have four leaves," Leo said as he walked past her towards the gate.

Julie stared at the two sets of four leafed clovers she'd picked. "Just one is supposed to be lucky, can you imagine what luck hundreds will bring."

Leo didn't even look back. He held the gate open waiting for her to catch up. He muttered to himself under his breath. "Yes. The house is full of life's luckiest people, lottery winners one and all."

It took about twenty five minutes to walk to the arcade. Julie must have been out of condition because she was getting slower and slower as they walked. The name above the blacked out window read, 'The Arcade' in truth it was a converted shop that housed several slot machines and a number of arcade computer games. Many of the machines were out of order, and the man who sat in the glass booth who handed out the change had no personality and little interest in what was going on.

As they walked in, a couple of lads on a machine that involved shooting moving targets shouted 'Hello' to Leo. "This is my favourite," Leo said walking over to a large screen that had a kind of bucket seat positioned in front of it along with an array of dials, levers and buttons. "I hold all the records on this little beauty." The two other boys

Clover House

that had welcomed them came across to watch Leo as he took up position and adjusted the seat to his height.

Julie watched as the screen facing Leo filled with the view of the sky. Along the bottom she could see mountains and lakes. It was so realistic she felt she could have been on a flight deck of a fast moving jet. "Here we go," shouted Leo as explosions appeared to fill the false sky. He pushed forward on the control lever with his left hand, now it was the lake below that filled the screen. At the last moment he pulled back and the pretend aircraft was once again climbing, only this time another aircraft was directly ahead. Julie had to hold on to the back of his chair, she was starting to feel a little dizzy. Leo pushed the red button on the end of the lever and a line of dots began to travel towards the aircraft ahead. BANG!!!! The plane crossing their path exploded in a sea of colours, once again the other boys cheered. From nowhere came another jet and again the dog fight began.

Eventually Julie got bored and started wondering around looking at the other machines. Finding a coin in the tray beneath the one-armed bandit she took it out and fed it into the slot. The red numbers showed she had four credits. The dials spun each time she pushed the start button but it wasn't until the fourth go that it started flashing to show

Clover House

she'd won something. She looked over towards Leo and thought about sharing the fact that she'd won, but he was too engaged with his flight simulator to take any notice. She played that machine for another fifteen minutes before her winnings had all been put back in and all the credits had been used.

Julie never noticed the man leave his glass booth, the first thing she was aware of was his breath on the back of her neck. "I can get you free goes if you like."

She spun around to find him sneering at her through gaps in his teeth. Slightly panicked she rushed back to Leo and said, "I want to go now." He totally ignored her, all his concentration was on the Aerial Joust. "I said I want to go now," she repeated.

"Well go then. We aren't tied together." The two boys cheered as another of his adversaries spiralled out of control. Leo punched the air, "record score as well," he high-fived the onlookers. When the game finished he climbed out of the pilot's seat and looked around for Julie. She was gone.

Leaving the arcade he looked up and down the street to see which direction she'd gone. He could see her in the distance. He walked a bit faster than normal and that was all it took to catch up to his new companion. He could tell she was sulking. "You're used to getting your own way aren't you?" he asked.

Clover House

"No. I'm just not used to being ignored," she said petulantly.

"I didn't ignore you, I was busy," Leo said walking crab like alongside her. There was something about her that he liked. He couldn't put his finger on it, but in some way she was different. He would never have taken anyone else from the home to his precious arcade, especially a female. "So what's your story? Everyone has one."

Julie stopped in her tracks. "Maybe I have one but don't want to share it."

Leo felt a little hurt. "Fair enough, your choice," he said, not knowing what else to say.

Julie sighed. "Last year my father died and since then my mother, who isn't very well, has struggled to look after me. So I end up at Clover House without anybody asking my opinion." Leo had heard this story a thousand times from other residents. The one thing in common with everybody's story is that things seem to happen without you having any say in it.

"Don't you have any other family?" Leo asked showing genuine interest.

"I don't think so. Not that would be willing to take me on anyway," she replied. Leo thought this a curious thing to say. She seemed quite amiable, a little temperamental at times but not difficult.

Clover House

"What about you, what's your story?" she asked. In a way she seemed to be trying to change the subject.

"It's similar to yours," he said with a shrug of the shoulders, "a one parent family that can't cope, or doesn't care enough to want to. I came to Clover a long time ago, or so it seems." He continued walking but facing straight ahead now. His expression was that of someone who was a little lost or struggling to remember the past. He snapped back to the present. "When's your birthday?" Julie thought this a curious question and right out of the blue.

"July the seventh," she said humouring him.

Leo paused for a moment then said "That's in a couple weeks. That makes you a Cancer."

Julie froze. "What do you mean you bastard?" This caught Leo completely off guard. He repeated his last comment to himself in his head and wondered why she had taken offence.

He continued. "Your birth sign is Cancer. That means you're emotional. Which we've proved... and your lucky number is...number 5?"

"Oh. I see. No it's number 3. How come you know about these things I thought it was supposed to be girls that knew about things like that?" She released a glimmer of a smile that diffused the outburst.

Clover House

He smiled back. "I know a little bit about everything," then added. "I watch a lot of TV."

Julie started walking again. She turned to Leo and asked, "When is your birthday then?"

"Ah, well. Nobody has any excuse for forgetting my birthday," he said proudly. "You see my birthday is on.... get this, Remembrance Day. I was born on the 11th of November. So once you see everybody wearing the bright red poppies, you know it's time to go out and buy Leo French his birthday present."

"French? Your last name is French?" Julie repeated, extending the 'F' in the word to make it last twice as long as it should.

"What's wrong with that?" asked Leo appearing to take offence, "and before you ask. No I'm not."

"Nothing is wrong with it. I've just never heard anybody with that as a second name before. I think it's quite nice really." She quickly realised this sounded a little too eager so tried to redeem herself, "I'll call you Froggy."

"You'll call me Leo like everyone else or you don't speak to me." Leo smirked and walked off ahead pretending to be annoyed. Julie ran to catch up. Once alongside she matched him pace for pace. Leo was thinking of questions to keep the conversation going. "What's your favourite colour?" he asked.

Clover House

Julie thought for a moment. "Black," she said.

"Black isn't a colour, it's a contrast of light," Leo replied with authority.

"Don't tell me, you picked up that little morsel from the TV as well," Julie said. "Anyway, it's my favourite colour. What's yours?" she added.

Leo looked puzzled. He had just realised nobody had ever asked him this before. After contemplating the question for what seemed more than necessary he blurted out, "I don't have one. I like them all."

"Everybody has a favourite colour," Julie said thinking he was just being awkward.

"Not me," replied Leo. He appeared quite proud of his answer and inside he had filed that reply away to be used if ever the question was asked again.

"Favourite food?" he then asked her.

"Chips," this reply came without any thought and brought a big smile to Julie's face. "What's yours?" she countered.

Another puzzled look swept over Leo's face. He had entered new territory with this conversation. Never before could he remember anyone taking an interest in what he preferred, let alone asked the question out loud. "I think it's ice cream."

Clover House

Julie stared at him. "You think it's ice cream?" She didn't know if he was just being difficult on purpose.

"No. Now I think about it, I know it is ice cream."

Clover House
Chapter 3

It wasn't often that all the residents went on an expedition together but at least once a year they borrowed the minibus from Carton House in the north of Leeds and went to visit Crowther Farm. Although the farm was classed as a 'working urban farm', in truth most of its income came from the visitors that rolled up every day to see the animals up close and learn about traditional farming method

As always Mr Jacobs lined up the residents for a final inspection. He went down the line making sure they all had the correct footwear and waterproof clothing (not that he could do much about it if they hadn't) and to check that everyone had the packed lunch that Marge had prepared that morning.

"Leo, trainers are hardly appropriate footwear. Don't you possess any boots?"

"No sir, this is it." Mr Jacobs walked on shaking his head and wasn't completely surprised to find Julie next to him in similar attire.

Julie looked up and saw who she thought must be James and Dave joining the line. She knew instantly what Leo had been getting at when he described them, as they were both wearing clothes that could at best be described as unisex.

Clover House

Mr Green, whose job it was to drive today, beeped his horn as he pulled up outside the gate. "This is exciting," said Julie.

"You think so?" replied Leo who had been to the farm at least six times since he came to Clover House. "Don't get too excited. It's not that great."

The front door was opened and they all marched out and on to the minibus. Tommy claimed the back seat to himself and fortunately there were sufficient seats so that nobody had to join him. That was until Mr Jacobs climbed aboard and found that next to Tommy were the only vacant seats left. Even he accepted it hesitantly.

As they neared the farm, Fish pointed excitedly out of the window on their left. "Look, that cow is trying to get a piggy-back off that other one." They all turned and looked in that direction, a number of the residents burst out laughing.

"For a start, Fish, they are not both cows, you can see that the one behind has horns. Secondly he's not asking for a piggy-back he's trying to..."

Mr Green cut Leo short. "Maybe that is a discussion you two should have alone." Leo could see him watching him through the rear view mirror as he drove.

They pulled into the farmyard and parked the minibus in the allocated space. Everyone on board jumped to their feet. "Sit back down!" shouted Mr

Clover House

Jacobs, "I just want to remind you of a few rules whilst on the farm."

"Firstly, don't go wondering off the paths, there is no excuse, they are clearly marked. Secondly, we will all meet in the picnic area at 1pm behind the farm shop which is over there." He pointed out of the front window.

"Thirdly, please obey all the signs. Some of the animals you can pet and feed others you can only see at a safe distance." He looked directly at Fish before continuing, "For example, the bull."

Mr Green opened the doors to allow a member of the farm staff onto the bus. "Good morning everyone, my name is Carol. I will be your guide for today," said the young woman in the safari uniform. "You are the first group to arrive today so I am going to show you around and give you the opportunity for some 'hands on' experience." The residents had no idea what she was talking about. "After that you can have some free time to take a look around yourselves. Don't forget the farm shop, if you would like to purchase a souvenir we have everything from key rings to books about the farm and the animals that live here. I would like to point out that we do not charge visitors but the farm is kept going from the profit from the shop. Okay everybody, please follow me."

Clover House

They all got off the bus and formed a semi-circle around Carol. When they were all present she shouted, "Follow me," and marched off in the direction of a barn about thirty yards away.

Taking instruction from Carol they all gathered around a goat that was stood looking suspiciously at them between two other smaller goats. All had been tethered to the floor by a piece of old rope.

"Come a bit closer. I'm going to demonstrate how to milk a goat," said Carol.

"I thought milk came from cows?" asked Fish.

"All animals produce milk but it is usually cow's or goat's milk that people drink, or of course make into cheese." Carol was never surprised by the naivety of some of the visitors. In the past she even had one little girl who thought it just came from the local shop.

She positioned a small three legged stool at the rear of the animal and placed a bucket underneath it. "Watch carefully how I position my hands and fingers." She began to squeeze the goat's teat and small jets of milk were propelled in to the bucket below. "Who would like to have a go?" she asked.

Nobody volunteered so she stood up and placed a hand on Fish's shoulder, "How about you young man?"

Fish looked at Mr Jacobs with an expression that said 'do I have to?' Mr Jacobs nodded in reply.

Clover House

Taking instruction, Fish sat on the small stool and grabbed the goat's udder. "Be gentle," said Carol, she placed her hand over his and helped him produce the first squirt, after that he managed to do it on his own.

Tommy shouted from the back, "James, Dave you two should be good at this. I bet you practice on each other." They tutted and looked away knowing that any kind of reply would later result in some form of painful retaliation. The member of staff from the farm pretended not to have heard the comment.

After Fish had got the hang of it, she let him return to the group and asked if anybody else wanted a go. No one replied, so she looked across at Tommy and said, "You look like a big strong man, how about you having a go. Surely you're not afraid of a little goat?"

"I'm not afraid of anything, but I'm certainly not touching that manky looking thing, especially down there." Mr Green and Mr Jacobs looked at each other, almost waiting for Tommy to go off in one of his tempers.

Mary burst out with a question. "Is it right Miss that there are two glasses of milk in every bar of chocolate?"

"Well that's what the advert tells us, but of course that's cow's milk not goat's." Carol walked to the other side of the barn knowing that the group

Clover House

would automatically follow. "Over here we have some goat's cheese that you can try." They all wondered over to a long table that displayed the equipment used to produce the cheese.

She offered round a plate she had prepared earlier that contained small cubes of goat's cheese on cocktail sticks. Without anyone noticing, Mr Green had moved towards Tommy and was now stood right behind him. Over the time that Tommy had been at Clover House, the staff had learnt to recognise his mood changes that usually preceded a violent outburst. Mr Jacobs looked across at Tommy and whispered a silent pray, hoping Tommy would behave himself.

The response from the residents when trying the cheese was varied. The twins quite enjoyed the taste, even asking for seconds, whilst Mary immediately spit hers out and made pretend gagging noises. "Thank God they don't put this in chocolate," she said.

After the barn they all followed Carol out and across the yard to where half a dozen pigs were being housed in a fenced enclosure. "I'm not standing around here, it stinks," said Tommy wondering off. Mr Green followed him.

"What are they eating?" asked Leo.

Clover House

"This breed is called the 'Yorkshire' or 'Large White' pig. This is where your bacon may come from."

"Ours comes from Asda Miss," said Fish. She chuckled, then realised he wasn't joking.

"In answer to your question, what is it they are eating? Well that could be anything, because that's what pigs will eat, almost anything. Usually we feed them the scraps from the farm restaurant."

"How long would they live if we didn't kill them?" asked Julie.

"Usually between fifteen to twenty years. Another couple of interesting facts are that they are believed to be about as intelligent as a three year old child and regardless of how dirty and smelly they appear they are very clean animals. They never go to the toilet where there is food or where they sleep."

Leo stepped forward. "I once saw a TV program that said pigs are almost identical to humans."

"I've seen how you eat Leo, I can believe that." Even Julie laughed at this remark from Fish.

"No, he is right. The internal organs of a pig are very similar to a human's. One day in the future when you have a heart problem, it may even be replaced with a pig's"

"Have you already had this operation Mary?" asked Leo

Clover House

Julie said, "Don't be cruel Leo that's not very funny," though it did get a laugh from some of the others.

"Let's go and meet some chickens," said Carol. They all moved a little further down the yard where they found a pen containing several chickens and a large cockerel.

"These are the hens," said Carol pointing over to a group pecking away at some seeds that had been spread around the floor. "And the large one over there, that is the cock or rooster."

In a voice that only the group could hear, Leo said, "Miss, I think you will find that the big cock is over there." They all looked to see where he was pointing with his thumb over his shoulder. In the distance you could see Mr Green arguing with Tommy. Again Carol pretended not to have heard the comment. Mr Jacobs had to put a hand over his mouth and fake a cough to prevent anybody seeing him smiling.

Changing the subject swiftly Carol announced, "each hen can lay an egg a day."

"That must keep the cock busy Miss," said Leo.

"Ah well, that is a myth. You see, a hen will still lay its eggs even if a rooster (she decided a name change was in order) isn't present, but if you want to raise chicks from the eggs, then the rooster needs to visit the hen first."

Clover House

Leo turned to Julie. "Well I've heard it been called some things in my time but never 'a visit'."

"Is that another cock Miss?" They all turned to see what Fish was talking about. Carol closed her eyes and sighed. Mr Jacobs mouthed the words 'sorry' to her. Behind the barn they'd been in with the goats was a horse tied to a tree, a rather well-endowed horse.

"Jesus Christ almighty!" said Mary as she stood mouth agape.

"That's Mr Ed, you can go and stroke him," she quickly corrected herself. "I mean feed him, in your free time after we've seen the farm machinery.

Carol marched off, guiding them to yet another barn: this one housed all kinds of farming implements from a combined harvester to bee-keeping equipment.

This didn't interest the residents much so Carol decided to cut the accompanied part of the tour short and let them start exploring the farm themselves.

They all ran out of that barn like a set of crazed lunatics, all going in different directions. For some reason Mary headed straight for Mr Ed. Leo and Julie walked over to a large pen that contained various breeds of rabbits. There was a sign that said you were allowed to go inside and handle the rabbits but must close the gate behind you.

Clover House

Julie stepped carefully over the smaller ones to a large white rabbit that looked like it belonged on the set of 'Alice in Wonderland'. "Look at the size of this one," she said trying to pick it up. It was much too heavy for her so she decided to just kneel next to it and stroke it.

Leo wasn't really an animal lover, he had a vague memory of his mother having a dog some time ago, but it seemed just a distant memory and he couldn't even remember its name. Julie was completely different all the rabbits seemed to flock to her. They say that animals have an instinct for people, and on this one he was with the rabbits. The more time he spent in Julie's company the more she grew on him.

After visiting all the animals it was time to head for the Visitor Centre. This building with the rather ambitious name was basically a converted barn that housed a small gift shop and a canteen. Leo wasn't really interested in the shop because he'd been numerous times before. His mind was on the picnic area round the back where Mr Jacobs said they were supposed to meet at 1pm. He was starving, but he didn't want to upset Julie who appeared to be in her element. She was scrutinising every trinket and souvenir in the shop. She was looking at the key fobs for what felt like ages. She was handling each one

Clover House

and reading all the little mottos that were encased in the tiny plastic squares.

"Are you not hungry yet, Julie?" This was the most tactful way he could think of getting his message across, what he really wanted to say was, "Julie, for Christ's sake put down the cheap tack and let's go and get some food."

She accepted the hint and replaced the rabbit-foot lucky charm on to its hook. She was a little concerned that the farm would sell such an object when only five minutes ago she was surrounded by the beautiful creatures. Were they being raised to be made into lucky charms? No, surely not.

Leo and Julie were the last of the group to arrive at the rendezvous point. The rest had opened their packed lunches and were silently chomping away on the savoury delights put together by Marge's fair hands. Mr Green had taken a crate of Coca-Cola from the back of the minibus and was handing them round. Leo couldn't help but notice that Tommy had a table all to himself.

Julie and Leo joined Fish and Mary at their table. "It's quite cool here, don't you think so Leo?" asked Fish.

"Thinking of becoming a farm worker then Fish?" joked Leo.

Clover House

"No actually I was just thinking, how come Carlton House has its own minibus and we don't. If we had one we could go on trips like this all the time."

"There is a reason they have a bus and we don't." Both Julie and Mary put their sandwiches down, waiting to hear the explanation. "Who decides where all the money is spent?" asked Leo.

They all thought for a moment before Mary offered an answer. "Mrs Westland?"

"And guess where her sister is Deputy Manager?" asked Leo.

Julie asked, "Would that be Carlton House by any chance?"

"Coorrrect! The lucky lady gets any prize from the top shelf."

"But that can't be right, it's not fair," complained Julie.

"Welcome to the unfair world of Social Services," said Leo.

The conversation was interrupted when somebody from another party tried to sit at Tommy's table. He left them in no doubt that it was his table and nobody else's, using some pretty choice language along the way. Mr Jacobs went straight to the victim of Tommy's abuse and tried to placate them with his apologies. Tommy just continued to eat his food like nothing had happened.

Clover House

"He's horrible," said Julie.

"That's why I told you to stay out of his way, he can be a touch unpredictable," replied Leo.

"Can't they do something about him?" asked Julie with her nose turned up in disgust.

"What like send him away to another home? That would just be passing the problem on to someone else."

After lunch they all returned to the minibus. Mr Green was waiting at the door to check everybody's shoes. He was responsible for the minibus so didn't want to be the one who had to clean up any of the mess that was brought on board under anyone's shoes. If he thought anybody looked suspect, he made the person go and scrape their shoes on the grass, giving them a further inspection before getting on.

Julie was one of those sent to the grass but once she was back on the bus she made straight for the vacant seat next to Leo. "Thanks for saving my seat," she said.

"I didn't," said Leo. Julie felt embarrassed for making the assumption.

"Only kidding," said Leo. "Of course I saved it." She smiled and sat a little closer to him than she needed to.

Mary shouted from the back of the bus, "Mr Green. I think Wee Willy needs the toilet."

Clover House

"What makes you think that Mary?" he asked nervously.

"Strike that Mr Green, he doesn't need it anymore," shouted Mary.

When they arrived back at Clover House, it took Mr Green an hour to clean and dry where Willy had been sitting and an excessive amount of air spray to disguise the smell.

Clover House
Chapter 4

They arrived back at Clover House just before the evening meal. Leo opened the gate and moved to the side to let Julie pass through first. A large over bearing woman forced Julie out of the way as she pushed through the open gate.

"Well excuse me!" Julie shouted at the woman's back as she marched down the path to a parked car.

The woman froze and began to turn ever so slowly. Leo looked across at Julie and gave her a frown and the tiniest shake of his head. The woman walked back to the gate. "Were you talking to me?" she asked Julie, almost daring her to answer. Julie gave a sideways glance at Leo. Again he gave the minute movement of his head from side to side.

"No," replied Julie, "my friend here." she nodded in the direction of Leo. The woman looked across at Leo as if he was something unpleasant she had just stood in, and without a word turned and continued the short journey to the parked car.

"What was all that about?" asked Julie seething, "and who the hell was she?"

"That's Mrs Westland. She's a right cow but trust me you don't want to get on the wrong side of her. My mate 'Si' gave her a mouth full one day, by the end of the week he was gone?"

Clover House

"Gone? Gone where?" asked Julie wearing a puzzled expression.

"That's it. Nobody knows. One day he was here and the next he was gone."

"How do you know it had anything to do with her?" She asked.

"Well... I don't, but it was a hell of a coincidence." Leo turned to walk away. Julie spun him back to face her with a pull of his sleeve. "You said who she is, but not what she's doing here."

Leo looked down at where Julie held his sleeve and she let go. "She's the boss of all the homes in Leeds, the one I was telling you about. Well, not the boss exactly but she's in charge of the finances anyway. She decides who gets what. Well that's what I've heard. She even says how much spending money we get."

"Spending money?" until this point Julie hadn't thought about money, she just presumed everything was supplied by the home. Leo had already turned around and was walking passed Mary, who was sat on the lawn eating a large bar of chocolate. He paused with the door open waiting for Julie to catch up.

"In answer to your next question, I don't know what everyone else gets but I receive £20 a week. Half of which I save the other half I usually spend down at the arcade."

Clover House

As Julie entered the house she asked over her shoulder, "what are you saving for, a rainy day?"

Again this was a question that Leo had never even asked himself. After a few seconds of deliberation he replied, "I don't know. When the time comes, then I'll know." Julie thought this to be a ridiculous answer.

The next day when they entered the dining room almost everybody else was seated and waiting to be served.

She moved around the table and sat in the seat she'd been allocated and Leo went straight through into the kitchen to give Marge a hand. "Thank goodness you are here Leo. For some veason I am rushed off my feet today."

Leo picked up the large plate of sausages and carried it through the swing doors to the waiting diners. As always it was two each but as he gave Tommy his share he grabbed Leo's wrist and said, "I'm hungry today, I want three sausages." Leo hesitated and looked up to see all eyes on him, including Julie's. There were no members of staff at the table and that meant no one to stand up to this bully or help out if things turned nasty. Leo plunged the fork into another sausage, wishing it was Tommy's head, then, placed it on the plate next to

41

Clover House

the other two. Out of the corner of his eye he could see Julie shaking her head in disappointment.

After serving everyone else he put the remaining single sausage on his own plate. Marge entered the room and distributed the mash potato, she placed two large gravy boats in the centre of the table and left. The rest of the meal was eaten in silence.

What remained of the afternoon was like all the other Saturday afternoons that Leo could remember. There was an argument taking place over the two computers, well one computer actually. Tommy was using one so two of the lads were fighting over the other one. Fat Mary was sat in a corner reading a book and chomping on another delight made by Mr Cadbury and Wee Willy watched as the twins sat at the coffee table dealing cards. The rest of the residents and staff were watching the TV as the new one had been delivered and installed, of course this resulted in a disagreement about which channel should be watched.

Leo was feeling down and still a little embarrassed over the confrontation at lunch. His heart lifted a little when Miss Stevenson entered the room. She set up her makeshift chemist on a small table in the corner and called out names for people to come and receive any medication they had been

Clover House

prescribed. It always astounded Leo the amount of residents that were on something.

Later, as Miss Stevenson began packing her medication away, she looked up and saw Leo looking at her. He smiled and she returned it. He lifted himself from his chair and walked towards her. She looked down at his leg as his limp was a little more exaggerated today, "Hi Leo. What can I do for you?" A little devil sat on Leo's left shoulder muttered something most inappropriate in his ear, he ignored it, "It's a little embarrassing," he said, his face flushing slightly.

"Would you rather discuss it somewhere more private?" she asked as she surveyed the busy lounge.

"If you don't mind," he replied.

They went off into the adjacent office without anyone noticing, he stepped in first, she followed and closed the door behind her. "Right Leo, what can I help you with?"

"I think I have a lump," he said. Miss Stevenson's face went all serious, her eyebrows dipped into a frown. "Where is it Leo? Would you prefer to see a male...?

"No I don't think it's anything like that it's.....on my bum." He slumped his head and wondered how much more embarrassment could one person take in a day. He turned and lowered the back of his trousers.

Clover House

Miss Stevenson took a step closer and lowered her reading glasses from her forehead on to the bridge of her nose. "Ah I see. It looks like an in growing hair that has produced a boil, nothing to worry about Leo. I'll give you some antibiotics and if it doesn't go down within a week, we'll look at draining it." She lifted her case onto the table and started looking for the right bottle. "It used to be called 'Jeep drivers' disease during the war. The soldiers in the desert would get it from driving and sweating down there all day. Here we are." She checked the label on a bottle, she held it up and began to shake two tablets into the palm of her hand.

"There is one other thing," Leo added with hesitation. "I have another lump." Miss Stevenson put down the bottle she was holding and wondered if this was the real reason he wanted to see her. "It's down there." Leo nodded down between his legs without taking his eyes off hers.

"Like I said Leo you can go to a male doctor if it's to do with down there." She nodded just like Leo had.

"It's more at the top of my leg," he replied, and without any hesitation removed his belt and lowered his trousers. "Just there," he said pointing where his thigh met his groin.

Clover House

"I think I know what that is... may I?" Miss Stevenson slid her hand over the area Leo had pointed out. She could feel a small lump exactly the size and in the position she had expected. She removed her hand just in time. As she had been moving her hand back and forth the knuckles of her fingers had been slightly touching Leo's testicles and he could tell that that wasn't the only lump he'd have to deal with if she'd have carried on.

She went over to a basin in the corner of the room and began washing her hands. "That's nothing to worry about Leo. You have a gland in the body in that area and the swelling is where it has gathered the badness created from the boil on your backside."

Leo let out a large sigh. This had been bothering him all week and like most males he was just ignoring the problem. Miss Stevenson dried her hands, closed her medical case and moved towards the door. "I'll check how you are next week Leo. As I said if it doesn't go down then it's just a case of some minor surgery, nothing at all really."

"Minor surgery?" Leo looked down at his privates.

Miss Stevenson smiled, "On the back bit Leo. Not the front bit. I must go now as I'm running late."

Within the next ten seconds three things happened all at once. Miss Stevenson opened the office door to leave, Leo began pulling up his

Clover House

trousers and to fasten his belt, and Julie walked into the lounge directly opposite the office door. When Leo looked up he saw her stood frozen to the spot with her mouth open. She spun around on one foot like a ballerina and stormed out of the lounge towards the stairs. It took Leo a second or two to realise what had just happened. He watched as Miss Stevenson left the lounge and finished fastening his belt. He smiled. A little pleased with himself that such a situation would have that effect on Julie. "Maybe she's a little jealous," he whispered, his smile growing wider. He decided to give Julie a while before explaining what she had really seen. He was quite flattered that she was so concerned. She'd laugh when she heard the truth.

Twenty minutes of watching a chick-flick on the new TV was all Leo could stand. It was only being shown because an argument between the residents about what to watch had resulted in a vote, James and Dave wanted one side, Leo and Fish the other. The deciding vote swung it James and Dave's way when Fat Mary had been persuaded to put down her book and join their camp. Leo decided to find Julie and put her mind straight about him and Miss Stevenson's illicit affair.

He climbed the steps carefully so as not to aggravate his leg. Julie's room was at the end of the corridor on the first floor. He approached the room

Clover House

quietly in case she was sleeping. The door was slightly ajar so he guessed she wasn't. He could see through the gap that she was sat on the bed with her back to him. He raised his hand to knock before entering but stopped, his hand poised in mid-air.

He couldn't believe what he was seeing. Julie was holding a syringe up, tapping the side to make any bubbles surface towards the needle. She gave it a final shake then pushed on the plunger ever so slightly making a thin squirt of liquid shoot out of the end of the needle. She repositioned herself on the bed, lifted her skirt as high as she could then pressed the needle deep into her thigh. Her shoulders raised with the pain as she pushed the plunger as far down as it would go, emptying all of its contents into her leg. Leo took a step back.

Thinking she had heard something Julie swung her head around quickly in the direction of the door, nobody was there.

Leo walked slowly down the stairs, oblivious to the sounds and mayhem erupting in the lounge, "Hi Leo. Is everything okay?" Leo came out of his daze to find Mr Green standing right in front of him. "Err... yes....fine....I think so," he replied shaking his head. He walked passed Mr Green as though he wasn't there, opened the door leading to outside and started running, down the short path, through the

Clover House

gate and along the road. From the open door Mr Green watched Leo go. He started to shout something after him but gave up before he'd even opened his mouth. He made a mental note to speak to Leo later to ask what it was all about.

Clover House
Chapter 5

As Julie sat eating her evening meal she glanced at the vacant chair next to her. Over her shoulder Marge nudged her to one side to make space then scooped a ladle full, of what Julie guessed was some kind of stew, from a steel terrine into her empty dish. "So you two had a lovers tiff?" Marge waited for a reply but when none was forth coming she added, "that is vot they call it, is it not? "Julie looked offended. "It's the right phrase but if you're referring to Leo and me it certainly does not apply here." Marge chuckled to herself and moved on to serve the next diner.

Just as they were finishing dessert Leo walked in. Nobody looked up except Julie and Marge as she collected the dirty dishes. "Don't be thinking you vill get something to eat now. This isn't a buffet at Tesco's. You can't just come and go when you choose." He was about to do a U-turn when Marge called after him, "I am joking Leo. How is your day? Come sit down I vill find something for you."

"It's okay Marge, I'm not that hungry." Leo completed his turn and walked out the door. Marge turned and looked at Julie, expecting some kind of explanation. Julie just shrugged her shoulders. She was as puzzled as Marge.

Clover House

When Julie finally left the dining room she was surprised to find Leo sat alone on the sofa in front of the television. She sat down beside him. "Not hungry? Doesn't sound like you, is something wrong?" She waited for a response but Leo sat without moving, his eyes transfixed on the television. "Excuse me. Earth to Leo, Earth to Leo," again there was no reaction. "Is there something wrong, is it something I've said or done," she added. She wasn't sure but she thought she heard some kind of snigger. She sighed. "Okay if you don't want to talk to me that's fine, I'll just leave you alone." She stood up to leave hoping this would trigger some response.

Nothing.

Left alone in the lounge Leo debated what to do next. He liked Julie, in fact he liked her a lot but he had this thing about people who take drugs. He considered them weak and irresponsible. The people that sell the drugs were to Leo, the scum of the earth. He placed his elbows on his knees and sank his head into his hands.

"Are you sure you're alright Leo?" Leo physically jumped. He thought he was alone in the room. Stood right in front of him wearing a face full of concern was Mr Green. "I'm fine, just a few things on my mind," he lied there was only one thing on his mind and that was Julie.

Clover House

"They say a trouble shared and all that," said Mr Green, changing his concerned look to a big smile. Leo thought for a while. He didn't want to tell on Julie but then again he knew he had to do something.

"Mr Green, what do you know about drugs?"

The response from the member of staff standing over Leo was amazing. Gone was the cheery smile, his arms became quickly folded and he actually took a step back, as though he had just found out Leo had a contagious disease.

"Why are you asking?"

Any onlooker would have thought Mr Green had been asked a trick question. His none committal answer and defensive manner made it clear to Leo that he was speaking to the wrong person. "No reason at all. I've just been watching a programme about them on television," he replied trying to diffuse the situation.

Mr Green glanced at the television, then back to Leo. He looked like a judge sizing up a convicted man before handing over the sentence. "I know you should stay away from them, I know that much." Without another word he turned and marched out of the lounge.

Leo went over to the vacant computer terminal, next to him Johnny Fish was playing a game of football on the other screen. He brought up

Clover House

Google and held his fingers over the keyboard. Not knowing what to search for he typed the word DRUGS into the space and hit the enter button. The response he got was...

DRUGS AND DRUG ABUSE

DRUGS – Wikipedia

There was also a story about the leader of a drug cartel that had been found dead. Not the kind of help he was looking for. He decided to sleep on the problem and consider his options in the morning. One thing was clear in his mind, doing nothing wasn't an option.

The next morning Marge arrived at Clover House at her usual time. She liked to get the breakfasts on the go whilst most of the residents were still in bed so she made it a habit to be in the kitchen and started by at least 7am. Marge hummed a tune as she swapped her coat for her overall. She was just about to hang it on the back of the kitchen door when it swung open. "Jesus vept!!!" she called out as Leo put his head round the door and wished her good morning. "Vot is wrong viv you this morning, have you peed zee bed?" she said trying to regain her composure.

"No, I just couldn't sleep," replied Leo with a smile. "I thought you may need some help." Without saying a word Marge pointed to the washing up in

Clover House

the sink. When she leaves the kitchen in an evening it is always spick and span, however it was inevitable that when she arrived the next morning there would be some washing up to be done, residents would get peckish during the night and raid the kitchen for anything that wasn't locked away.

Leo did the washing up. He then moved on to drying the pots, setting the table, helped to serve the food and even cleaned everything away. The one thing he didn't do was sit at the table with the others for breakfast. Marge noticed this but said nothing. She saw him nibbling on a piece of toast as he went about his tasks but he remained silent throughout. Whilst he'd been serving the food Julie had tried to get his attention on more than one occasion, but he completely ignored her.

Leo waited for all the diners to leave before he stepped out of the kitchen. He checked they had all left through a gap in the door, hung up the apron he'd been wearing and walked across the dining room. The door opposite opened and Leo froze, he was praying it wasn't Julie. His prayers were answered when in walked Mr Green.

Mr Green walked up to Leo and before saying anything looked over both his shoulders to make sure they were alone. "I have something for you," he said before again looking over both his shoulders. Leo felt like a spy in a bad movie, he felt he should be

Clover House

offering Mr Green some kind of password in exchange for what he was about to be given. Mr Green slid his hand under his jacket and pulled out an envelope. "I hope these will be useful."

"Right...okay....thanks." Leo had no idea what could be in the envelope, but taking Mr Green's lead, he said thank you again, slid the envelope under his jumper, left the kitchen and headed for his bedroom.

He closed the bedroom door, sat on the bed and retrieved the envelope from underneath his jumper. He slid his finger under the gap at one end and ran it across the top to tear it open. He peaked inside then turned the envelope upside down allowing its contents to spill out on to the bed. An assortment of leaflets and information sheets about the use and dangers of various drugs stared up at him. Picking one at random he began reading about the side effects of taking marihuana. His knowledge of street drugs was limited but he was pretty sure you didn't inject that particular drug, he selected another sheet.

Over the next hour he read every word on every leaflet. The most useful ones gave advice on what to look for if you thought someone you knew was taking one of the drugs. They mentioned things like mood swings (Julie was a female so those were to be expected anyway), paranoia, sweating, being excitable etc. Under the heading 'Physical signs' it listed examples including puncture marks, blood shot eyes, bad teeth and even weight loss. Leo hadn't known Julie very long but she just didn't seem to fit into any of the categories talked about.

Though Leo had eaten a little toast at breakfast, he hadn't had anything to drink and was now beginning to feel quite thirsty. He decided to get a glass of milk from the kitchen. He jumped off the bed, something he regretted immediately as he landed on his bad leg, and opened his bedroom door. Without even noticing her poised with her hand ready to knock, Leo walked straight into Julie, winding her slightly. "I'm so sorry," he said putting his arm around her shoulders in an effort to comfort her.

"Ah, talking to me now are we?" Leo removed his arm and took a step back into the safety of his bedroom, banging the back of his legs onto the side of the bed. "What are those?" asked Julie looking past him at the envelope and leaflets that were scattered across the unmade bed.

Leo moved forward pushing Julie gently back and closed the bedroom door behind him. "It's nothing that concerns you."

"What the hell is your problem Leo?" Julie said, hands on hips, legs slightly apart. "I'm going nowhere until we have sorted this out." Leo tried to get past her but she made a side step to block his path. They

Clover House

stared at each other in silence for a good thirty seconds, eventually Julie resigned herself to the fact that she wasn't going to get any explanation from him so she moved out of his way and let him pass.

As he walked down the corridor Leo glanced over his shoulder, not to see if Julie was following him, he just wanted to make sure he had closed his bedroom door properly. He didn't want her to know he'd found out her secret.

Leo spent the rest of the morning at the arcade. He put most of that week's allowance into the aerial combat game he liked so much, alas he ended up being shot down in almost every battle. He just couldn't concentrate. Once his money had been used up he watched the others playing their games. He wandered from machine to machine, anything was better than having to go back to Clover House and confront Julie with what he had found out. He replayed endlessly how the conversation would go. Should he just come straight out with it and tell her what he'd seen? Should he just bring up the subject of drugs and see how she reacts? Or, should he just tell a member of staff what he'd seen and let them deal with the problem? No, that was just being a coward. As it turned out the decision was made for him.

Leo opened the door gently and stepped into the hall gingerly, almost tip-toeing towards the steps.

Clover House

"Leo French, my office. Now please." Mr Jacobs was stood with his arms crossed as if he'd been waiting all day for Leo to return.

"Who's in trouble now?" said Tommy as they walked passed him, in a childish sing-song voice. Leo ignored him and followed Mr Jacobs into the office marked 'Manager'. Sat to one side of the desk was Mr Green, head down, not wanting to make eye contact. "Take a seat Leo," said Mr Jacobs pointing towards the vacant chair on the other side of his large mahogany desk. "Mr Green has brought something to my attention, something that concerns me greatly." The Manager continued, "What do you know about someone taking drugs in this establishment?" Leo glanced at Mr Green who still refused any eye contact.

Leo quickly weighed up the pros and cons of confessing what he had seen. If he told what he knew then the decision of what to do about it would then be out of his hands, no longer his responsibility.

"I'm waiting Leo." It was clear Mr Jacobs couldn't be side stepped as easily as Julie.

"I saw someone...," he hesitated looking for the right words. "I saw someone taking drugs." He expected Mr Jacobs to explode, to storm around his office shouting expletives demanding names, times, dates. Instead he sat back in his chair took a deep breath and said simply, "I see." Even Mr Green lifted

Clover House

his head and looked around as though he might have missed something.

Mr Jacobs leant forward, steepled his fingers and said, "Obviously we can't allow this to happen at Clover House. We have a responsibility for everybody here, and if someone is taking a 'none prescriptive' drug, then as Manager, I have to do something about it."Leo swallowed nervously. He knew there would be repercussions but he didn't want Julie sent away, or even worse handed over to the police.

"Before I ask you for a name I want you to know Leo that nobody will learn of your involvement. I also want you to know that the person won't be dragged off to the nearest police station. My intention is to offer them all the support they need." Mr Jacobs ended with a rather patronising smile.

Leo understood that they had reached a point of no going back. What ever happened now was out of his control. He knew that Mr Jacobs wasn't going to rest until he had the details. He even picked up his pen, ready to write the offenders name on his desk pad. After a long pause Leo said with a broken voice, "It's Julie Sykes, Sir". He felt like Judas Iscariot. Mr Jacobs frowned, put down his pen without writing anything and looked sideways at Mr Green, who, in fact, was wearing the same puzzled look as his boss.

Clover House

"What did you see exactly? He asked, again leaning back into the deep leather of the high backed chair.

"I saw Julie with a syringe. She injected something into her leg." Leo's eye switched between the two men sat opposite him. This wasn't the response he was expecting, something was wrong. "Honest, it was the other day. She didn't know I was watching." He began to assume it was the fact that they didn't believe him that had produced this unlikely reaction. "I know Julie doesn't look like the kind, if there is a kind, but I swear Mr Jacobs, I'm not lying." Leo was starting to panic. If they didn't believe him then that means they would do nothing about it. Leo stood up quickly, almost knocking over his chair with the back of his legs.

"Leo, sit back down." When Leo didn't move Mr Jacobs added, "Please." Slowly he lowered himself back on to his chair he even pulled it forward a bit to its original position. "It's not that we don't believe you." Mr Jacobs was physically struggling to find the right words, he stuttered as he continued. "We err, I err, want to... err. This... is a delicate situation Leo." Before Leo could say anything Mr Jacobs rose from his chair and started walking around the small office. Eventually he stopped between Leo and the front of his desk. He leant back and folded his arms. "I think this situation would be

Clover House

better handled by someone else." He pushed himself upright, nodded towards Mr Green and headed for the door. Mr Green stood up quickly and left the office leaving Leo by himself.

It seemed like an eternity but was probably less than five minutes before the door swung open and in walked Miss Stevenson. Leo turned his swivel chair expecting to see Mr Jacobs. "I'm sorry Mr Jacobs has just stepped out." Hoping that would explain why he was sat alone in the Manager's office. Without a word Miss Stevenson walked passed Leo, around the large desk and lowered herself slowly into the leather seat.

"I've just had a word with Mr Jacobs and he's asked me to come and speak with you about what you witnessed the other day."

This was getting serious; she's even using legal terminology. Leo shuffled in his chair like a boy in front of the headmaster. "Look I know what I saw; I'm not making it up."

"I know what you think you saw, Leo." This was the last straw. Leo came to the conclusion that it was all going to be covered up, swept under the carpet, just so Clover House didn't have its reputation dragged through the papers. Well Leo French was having none of it. Again he stood up quickly, this time the chair did fall over behind him. He put the

Clover House

palms of his hands on the table and moved his face within inches of the woman facing him.

"I know what I fucking saw. There is a person upstairs in this building that needs help and if you lot aren't going to give her it then I'll find someone who will."

Miss Stevenson didn't bat an eyelid. Without retreating an inch she said calmly, "Leo. Sit back down. There is something I need to explain to you."

Leo turned picked up his chair and sat back down. With the back of his left hand he wiped away the spittle on his chin. Miss Stevenson shuffled some papers on the desk for something to do while Leo calmed down. "You need to speak to Julie," she said in a gentle, motherly voice.

Leo shook his head from side to side. "Great. Like she's ever going to admit it to me," Leo slapped his hands onto his thighs in dismay.

"Listen to me Leo," she continued, "Go upstairs now and tell her what you saw. Tell her that you have spoken to me and I suggested you discuss it with her."

"What do I do if she kicks off, or just denies it to my face?" a touch of anger still emanated in his voice.

"Leo, go now." As far as Miss Stevenson was concerned the conversation was over. Exasperated

Clover House

Leo grunted something and left the office, slamming the door behind him.

He made the journey from the office to Julie's bedroom last as long as possible, in an effort to prolong the inevitable confrontation they were about to have. It also gave him time to rehearse his opening statement. The time was cut short when he met Julie coming the other way down the short corridor. He stopped, straightened his back and smiled. She just walked past him as though he wasn't there. "Julie!" he shouted to the back of her head. She stopped but didn't turn around. "Can I have a word?" Leo said rather sheepishly. It took a while but at last she slowly turned. The expression on her face was blank, "in private?" Leo added and moved towards her bedroom door. He turned the handle and pushed it open waiting for her to join him. Julie walked like she didn't have a care in the world. Passing him, hidden from sight, she let a small smile flicker across her lips.

"Sit down, please. I have something to ask you." Julie did as she was asked moving some clothes out of the way she perched on the corner of the bed and waited for him to continue. Without any preamble Leo blurted out the question. "Julie, are you taking drugs?"

"Drugs?" what are you talking about Leo? Do I look like the kind of person that takes drugs?" She

Clover House

had no idea where this accusation had come from, but it certainly explained his behaviour over the last few days. Leo was expecting this denial. She was so convincing, not a flicker of guilt on her face. He knew that people who take drugs become well accustomed to lying.

His entire reason for asking her came out in a rush of words without any break for air. "I was stood at your door and saw you injecting something, I didn't know what to do but Mr Jacobs found out and asked me... and I said it was you. He then sent in Miss Stevenson who didn't believe me but asked me to come and ask you." He stood gasping, a combination of replacing the oxygen, nerves and fear.

"You were spying on me?" Within a second the tables had turned and for some reason he now felt like the accused.

"The other day I came here to tell you something, your door wasn't closed properly and I watched you. You even prepared the needle like a professional." A look of disgust hung on Leo's face. Julie lowered her eyes and stared at her hands on her knees, twiddling with her rings. She looked back up at Leo, smiled and then patted the space on the bed next to her.

"Please Leo, sit down." Leo wondered what the record was for being told to 'sit down' in one day.

Clover House

"What you saw was me taking my medication. I have to inject it into my thigh every day. It's part of my treatment."

Leo's mind flashed back to an auntie he had who used to inject insulin every day as part of the treatment for diabetes. "You're a diabetic?" This explained everything. Obviously Mr Jacobs knew all about it, that's why he wasn't surprised when Leo had given Julie's name. And why he'd asked Miss Stevenson to come into the office.

"No, I'm not diabetic, Leo." Again the smile disappeared and her eyes dropped back to her hands.

"I feel such an idiot," said Leo. "I bet everyone was laughing at me, as if you would even know how to take drugs." He let out a short laugh, but stopped when Julie placed her hand on his and raised her face. There was a single tear running down each of her cheeks.

"Leo...it's cancer." There it was out in the open. The one word in the English language that was guaranteed to take a smile off anyone's face, the one word that could stop any conversation. The one word that once uttered changed people's lives forever. Leo waited for the punch line, this had to be some kind of joke, a sick one at that but he would accept that rather than it being the truth. He sat there on the bed staring into space and shaking his head.

"But you're getting better, right?" He carried on speaking rather than hear the answer. "The treatment is working and you are going to be okay, yes? It's only a small cancer and they can deal with it, right?"

"No."

Leo stood up. Suddenly the small bedroom felt claustrophobic, he needed to get outside. He started rambling. "Why does it always happen to me? Every time I start getting close to someone they leave me." He looked back at Julie. "Oh my God, I'm sorry I'm being so selfish." He lowered himself onto the bed and put his arm around her. "How are you feeling? Does it hurt anywhere?"

"Leo, I have less than six months to live." She tried to force a smile but it didn't work, her lips were shaking too much. "It's okay. I have come to terms with it. The doctors have been great, they have tried everything so now it's just a matter of waiting." She used her thumb to wipe away the tear that was now running down Leo's cheek.

"How can you be so brave?" The question was dumb; in truth she didn't have any choice in the matter. "Why are you spending your last months on earth in this dump?

Clover House

"Like I said the other day, my mother isn't very well and what with my illness as well, she just can't cope. But hey, look on the bright side," Leo frowned. Could they possibly be a bright side to this situation? "I met you," she added. He smiled and placed his arms gently around her and kissed her cheek. "I don't want you treating me any different now you know, Leo. That's why I don't tell people. Suddenly they start treating you like you're an invalid and made out of glass. They even start speaking to you with a stupid voice like you've regressed to being four years old."

After several minutes they released each other. The side of Leo's face was damp from Julie's tears. "Right, if you have six months left..."

Before he could continue Julie corrected him, "less than six months Leo. The doctors gave me a year, that was eight months ago."

Leo brushed her comment aside as though it was an annoying fly, "Whatever. We are going to make this next six month...," he corrected himself, "...or however long it is, the best time Julie Sykes has ever had." Julie was so happy. She knew that Leo would find out one day soon about the cancer, but was worried how he would take it. This was better than she could have imagined or even dreamed of.

"What is on your bucket list?" Leo asked.

Clover House

"What's a bucket list?" Julie asked. She'd never heard the phrase before.

"A bucket list is a list of things you want to do before... you kick the bucket." Leo winced. He'd only ever seen the subject discussed on TV shows, usually comedies. Now speaking to someone who is actually going to die it seems a little heartless and such a blasé phrase.

Julie didn't take it that way she just continued the conversation. "I don't know what my bucket list is. I've never thought about it before." She placed her forefinger on her lip and began thinking.

"Don't just start mentioning things willy-nilly. This is important. Tonight I want you to think of all the things you would like to do. Things that you have always wanted to do but have either never got around to, or didn't think it was possible." Leo went over to the small desk in the corner of the room. He returned to the bed carrying a pad and a pen, he placed these on Julie's bedside cabinet. "There. Tonight I want you to have a serious think about it and to write them all down. I'm not a miracle worker but we'll see what we can do."

Clover House
Chapter 6

Leo was putting the plates on the table getting it ready for breakfast when in walked Mr Green. He came straight over to Leo. "Leo, I'm sorry about having to tell Mr Jacobs your secret."

"It's okay Mr Green. It's all worked out for the best. Julie told me about her...condition." Leo continued circling the table with the plates. He noticed a smudge on the next one he was about to put down, hesitated, realised it was Tommy Bishop's place and dropped it into position. "We had a long discussion about it last night. But seeing as you did reveal our secret I think you may owe me a favour or two." Mr Green smiled. He liked Leo so would have done him a favour without it being a means of payback.

"That sounds fair, Leo. As long as it's nothing against the House rules or doesn't cost me anything." Leo put down the last plate and looked up.

"Can't guarantee that Mr Green, but I'll bear it in mind." They nodded to each other and Mr Green left the dining room looking a lot happier than when he'd entered.

Everybody seemed to arrive at breakfast together. They all jockeyed for position, even though they knew their seats were allocated and had been

Clover House

the same ones since they arrived at Clover House. Leo was keen to get sat down next to Julie so on this occasion he left the serving of the food to Marge.

Leo sat down and tucked his napkin into the top of his jumper. He realised a long time ago that he was the only person around the table to do this, but it was something he'd always remembered doing, so what the hell. He turned to face Julie and asked nonchalantly, "did you manage to start your list?"

"You mean my bucket list?" said Julie, removing a scrap of folded paper from her jeans pocket.

"Let's not call it that," said Leo. "I don't think it sounds very nice. Let's call it your wish list." Julie smiled. She unfolded the paper and laid it on the table rubbing the palm of her hand over it in an effort to iron out the creases.

"What's that Frenchy, a love letter?" Tommy shouted across the table waiting for the laughter he normally got from his little quips, not because they were funny, it just felt safer if you were in striking distance.

"No it's not Tommy, but then again you wouldn't know what one looks like would you?" Leo knew that he would inevitably pay for this but at the moment he felt invincible. Tommy looked around the table almost daring anybody to laugh at Leo's come back.

69

Clover House

Julie scooped the piece of paper off the table and returned it to her pocket. She looked at Leo and whispered. "I'll show you it later." Leo smiled and nodded.

They had decided to go to the arcade that morning. The house was quite busy now it was summer and most of the residents were just hanging around bored. At this time of year there was no such thing as privacy. Leo knew of a small cafe on the way that they could use to discuss Julie's wish list.

They chose a seat at the back in the corner, not that there was much chance of them bumping into anyone they knew here but it looked more private and more appropriate for what they were about to discuss. Leo ordered two coffees and Julie corrected him saying she wanted a tea as there was something in coffee that she wasn't supposed to have. They chatted about nothing important until the drinks arrived. Julie suggested Leo watches his back after making fun of Tommy at breakfast.

The drinks were delivered by the same person that took the order, a rather overweight man in a stained overall. He lowered them onto the table letting a little spill from each. Neither Leo nor Julie even noticed. They were too excited about the list being ironed out on the table as it was at breakfast. Leo leaned forward but before he could read

Clover House

anything Julie snatched it up and held it to her chest. "Hey, this is private," she said teasing him.

"Well I thought that's why we were here, to go through it?" It was Leo's turn to wear the face of a disgruntled teenager.

"It is but I've made notes on it as well, some I might not want you to see." She swivelled sideways and held the sheet out so she could read it out without him being able to see it.

"How many are on the list?" asked Leo, the suspense almost killing him.

"Six at the moment, but it's a work in progress so there maybe more. Ready?" Julie took a deep breath.

"Fire away." Leo smiled and made himself comfortable whilst taking a sip from his coffee.

"Number one...," Julie looked a bit sad and Leo hoped that this wasn't going to be too much for her. "I want to visit my father's grave," then she added, "I've never seen it." She paused and looked up at Leo for a response.

"You've never seen it? Didn't you go to his funeral?" Leo asked, surprised.

"I was in hospital having treatment at the time. I was too ill. I know he was buried in Horsforth near the large roundabout but that's it."

Clover House

Leo thought for moment before saying, "I think I know which graveyard it is. That shouldn't be too difficult to arrange. What's next?"

Julie looked back at the piece of paper, she giggled and smiled. Leo liked to see her like this, he couldn't imagine what she was going through inside. "I want to go and see 'The Living Zombies'," she announced with gusto. Leo could tell that this had obviously been something she'd wanted to do for some time.

Leo returned her smile and said, "Fine... but who, or what the hell are The Living Zombies?" He shrugged his shoulders in defeat, he had never heard of them.

Julie made a little distance between them, put down the paper she was holding, held the bottom of her t-shirt with both hands and pulled it taught. "Derr!" she said. Leo looked at the print on the front of her t-shirt. It showed three skeletons holding guitars and a forth singing into a floor standing microphone that looked very much like the scythe the Grim Reaper carries.

His eyes drifted up to meet hers, again he shrugged his shoulders. "Oh my God, where have you been living for the last five years, a cave? This is the best rock band ever." All at once it dawned on Leo.

Clover House

"Ah, it's a rock band." Her comment about where he had been for the last five years left him embarrassed. He'd never really been into music that much, especially not rock music. "So you want to go and see this band?" he asked.

Julie looked a little forlorn. "Well you did ask me to write down everything I wanted to do."

Leo tried to rescue the situation. "Of course I did, and I promised to see what I could do." This was going to be tougher than he had first thought. He didn't want to disappoint Julie, but then again he was beginning to think her expectations may be a little high. He was starting to worry what else would be on the list.

"What's number three?" he said smiling.

"I want to touch the shadow of a palm tree in the sand.

There was a pregnant pause between them before Leo broke it by saying. "I'm sorry can you repeat that." Julie repeated what she had said and waited for him to respond. Leo thought for a few seconds and said, "That one's easy," Julie smiled. "There is a garden centre on the ring road we should be able to do it there."

A look of disappointment swept over her face. "I was kind of hoping I could do it in a foreign country... on a real beach."

Clover House

This was getting better and better Leo thought. He hadn't really thought this through when he suggested the idea but now it was all getting completely out of control, it was all going to end in disappointment. As though Julie had read his mind, she screwed up the piece of paper, threw it into the ash tray and announced, "I'm being stupid, I'm sorry. It's just that when you suggested writing down all the things I wanted to do, these are what came out. It all seemed so exciting...so possible." She started to cry and this felt to Leo like it was his entire fault. He felt like he was ripping her heart out.

He retrieved the paper, dusted off the ash and flattened it out again. He smiled and held it out for her, "...and number four?"

She looked down at the list. "This one may sound a little weird." Leo thought it couldn't be any weirder than the palm tree thing.

"I want to go skinny dipping." She lowered her head shyly.

"Like, go swimming with no clothes on?" Leo couldn't believe his ears. "Alone?" he asked wearing his famous cheeky grin.

"Leo French. What kind of girl do you think I am?" It was Julie's turn to wear the mischievous grin.

Leo smiled and said, "Maybe we could do it on the beach after we've touched the palm tree shadow."

Clover House

Julie's face changed in an instant. "If you're going to be sarcastic, we'll forget all this now." She started to rise from her chair. Leo pulled her back down and spent the next five minutes apologising.

"Number five?" Leo asked trying to change the subject. Eventually Julie sat back down and took a drink of tea. "I want to get drunk. Not crazy drunk, just tipsy." Leo thought about adding this to the beach trip and the skinny dipping. They could do three of the wish list in an hour. Fortunately, he had become quite attached to his manhood and presumed suggesting this to Julie would end in him being separated from it, so he just smiled and nodded. Out of all the things she had put on the wish list this one seemed the most doable. Getting hold of alcohol at Clover House had never been a problem.

"...and finally. What is number six?" Leo asked, though in truth he'd lost interest in the whole idea, he had about zero chance of pulling off half of what she had requested so far. Julie's lips moved but nothing came out. It was like she was rehearsing how to say it in her head without the words reaching her mouth. "You asked me to think of them and write them down Leo, nobody said I had to tell you them all."

"How can I help you achieve them if I don't know what they are?" he asked.

Clover House

"I told you some of them are private. Maybe there are some things I just have to sort out myself." She slipped the paper back into her pocket and finished her tea in one gulp. "Are we going to the arcade or not?" Without waiting for an answer she stood up and walked towards the door, leaving Leo to settle the bill.

Leo caught up with her a few yards down the road. He wasn't really in the mood for the arcade now; his mind was racing through the wish list. He was trying to find the words to use that would let Julie down without her being too disappointed. Before he realised, they had arrived. Julie entered the building first and went straight over to Leo's favourite game. He was pleased she took an interest in, I suppose you'd call it, his hobby. What he didn't expect was her to take position in the seat and start toying with the controls. "What are you doing?" he asked. Her hands were moving the joystick side to side and her feet were going up and down on the rudder pedals like she was using a foot pump.

"You don't think I'm going to spend all afternoon just watching you, do you? I want you to show me how to do it."

"It will take a while," he said thinking she would lose interest quickly.

Clover House

"We have all afternoon. What do these do?" she replied pushing buttons and flicking switches on the simulated aircraft flight panel.

Leo couldn't remember having as much fun as he had that afternoon. Going back to Clover House they laughed as they walked and Leo teased her about flying the way most women drive. Arriving back they were greeted by Tommy Bishop who stood at the gate like a sentry. "I think we have some unfinished business, Frenchy." The last thing Leo wanted was to take a beating in front of Julie. He certainly didn't want to look like a coward, so he stepped forward, expecting the inevitable.

"Excuse me gentlemen," said Mr Green as he walked between them and through the gate. Leo recognised his opportunity to kill two birds with one stone. He followed Mr Green calling after him. "Mr Green, can I have a word please?" He glanced over his shoulder to find Tommy Bishop snarling and mouthing the words "Later Frenchy."

Julie followed them into the house and tugged on Leo's sleeve. "I'll see you later Leo, I just need to do my medication thingy." She smiled and added, "Thanks for this afternoon, I had a great time," before scurrying up the stairs.

"Mr Green, you live in Horsforth don't you?

Mr Green nodded hesitantly and said, "yes,

why?"

As Julie entered the TV lounge Leo jumped up from the chair in front of the television and dashed across the room. He was wearing a massive smile and for some reason looked as pleased as punch with himself. "You look like the cat that's got the cream," said Julie as he dragged her into the hall. Leo looked around to make sure nobody could hear them.

"I've done it," he said offering no further explanation.

"Done what?" asked Julie completely oblivious to what he was talking about.

"Number one on the wish list, I've organised it for tomorrow lunch time." Julie was taken by surprise at how quickly Leo had acted on her requests. In fact it took her a few seconds to recall what number one on the list had been.

When she remembered what it was she was immediately overcome with excitement. "My father's grave? You've organised going to see it already?" She clapped her hands together like a small child.

"Mr Green lives over that way and he said he will drop us off when he goes home for lunch tomorrow, but we will only have about forty-five minutes or so." Julie threw her arms around Leo's neck and slapped the biggest kiss on his cheek that Leo's could ever remember receiving.

"Leo, you're unbelievable." She planted another kiss on his cheek and as she released him gave him the softest, most gentle kiss on the lips. The kiss probably only lasted half a second but it sent a shudder through Leo's body like never before.

For the rest of the day Leo didn't walk anywhere that was for mere mortals. No, Leo floated. He was happier than he had ever been, and if that was the response he got for completing just one of Julie's wishes, well, he was certainly going to do his upmost to deliver each and every one of them.

As he walked past the computer terminals he slapped Tommy Bishop on the back and said, "how's it going Tommy old boy?" which didn't go down well as it made him loose a life on the game he was playing, but as Mr Jacobs was strolling around at the same time Leo knew there would be no retaliation.

Clover House
Chapter 7

Mr Green's Ford Escort must have been at least fifteen years old and that was probably the last time it had been cleaned, but if this got them to where they wanted to go, then you wouldn't hear any complaining from the two passengers in the back seat. "I'll drop you off at the main gate to the cemetery and will pick you up thirty minutes later. I'm sorry Leo, but that's all the time I have today. If I hadn't already promised you then I wouldn't have even bothered going home for lunch today."

"That's fine Mr Green. We appreciate the trouble you're going to." Mr Green looked at the couple in his rear view mirror and smiled to himself. What he couldn't see was that they were holding hands in the space between them.

Leo nudged Julie as the cemetery came into view when they went over the brow of a small hill. She leant towards him so she could see through the gap between the two front seats. For some reason she felt a little nervous. Leo sensed this and gave her hand a squeeze.

The car came to rest right outside the large, wrought iron gates that were the main entrance to the grounds; the church was an impressive structure, towering over and above all the surrounding buildings. Leo opened his door and got out. Julie slid

Clover House

along her seat to get out of the same door. Just before pulling away Mr Green wound down his window and shouted a reminder. "Remember, I'll be back in thirty minutes." He then drove off without waiting for a reply.

Leo and Julie stood shoulder to shoulder. Still holding hands Leo looked at her and asked, "Are you okay? If you don't want to do this, that's fine, we'll just wait here for Mr Green to return."

"No, I'm ready," she replied and started walking along the long, winding path that gave access to all the burial plots.

"Do you have any idea where your father's buried?" asked Leo as he took in the hundreds of grave stones, some new, some ancient and decrepit. If they only had thirty minutes it was going to be a struggle to check them all in an effort to find just one.

"I remember my mother saying something about it being in the shade of some trees, and the only trees I can see are over in that corner." She nodded to a distant corner of the cemetery where a number of oak trees grew. They headed in that direction, picking up their pace, both aware that time was precious.

Once there, they split up and started reading the names carved on each stone. What surprised Leo was the number of younger people there were.

Clover House

Some of them even had photos built into the stone, only the recent ones had flowers.

"Over here," shouted Julie. Leo looked up to see her sat on a wooden bench staring at one of the head stones. He strolled over, sat down next to her and started reading the inscription on the large marble stone. It gave the usual details of name and dates and a short verse of how he will always be remembered. Leo could see a tear making its way down Julie's face.

"What was he like?" asked Leo.

Julie smiled. "He was a kind man and he loved me and my mother very much. He would often bring us presents back from his business trips." She held up her wrist to show a silver bracelet that had several charms attached. "He brought me this from Africa." Leo looked at it closely.

"What did he do, as a job I mean?"

Julie thought for a minute before answering. "Actually I'm not sure. He travelled a lot and we were never short of money, but now you ask. I don't know."

"Maybe he was a spy or worked for the Government as some kind of agent," said Leo pulling his jacket across his face so only his eyes showed above the lapel. She gave him a look that made him feel immature. "Sorry," he said lowering his jacket. "You never know, he might have been," he said in his

Clover House

defence. Julie continued to gaze at the headstone in silence.

Fifteen minutes past when Julie caught Leo checking his watch. "I suppose we should go now," said Julie.

"No rush. Take as long as you like," said Leo smiling and taking her hand in his again.

"Thank you," she said, returning his smile. Just then something shiny caught her eye. She stood up, bent down and picked it up, she returned to her seat rubbing the dirt and mud from its surface.

"What's that?" asked Leo. Once she'd cleaned it Julie passed it to him. It was a 50p piece.

"Look at the back of the coin," said Julie "You like planes, you have it." Leo took a closer look then turned the coin over. The engraving depicted three airmen running to their aircraft as the sky above them is filled with Bombers. The date on the bottom was 1940. It was a commemorative coin remembering the Battle of Britain. "I heard these had been in circulation but I've never seen one." Leo offered the coin back.

"You have it. Call it the price of my cup of tea the other day." Leo accepted the gift, put it to his lips, kissed it and said, "I'll never spend this, it will always remind me of you." He tucked it safely away into his jeans pocket.

Clover House

When the thirty minutes were up Julie stood, took the few steps to her Father's head stone and mumbled something Leo couldn't hear properly, it sounded like "May God be with you." She then kissed the tip of her fingers and touched them gently on to the top of the stone before whispering something else. She turned and held out her hand for Leo to take. He joined her and they walked slowly back to the entrance of the cemetery. Mr Green was parked waiting for them with the car engine running but he didn't say anything about them being a little late. "Is everything okay?" he asked.

Julie squeezed Leo's hand and said, "Couldn't be better Mr Green, couldn't be better.

On the morning of Julie's birthday, she came down the stairs totally unaware of what was waiting for her. It was tradition at Clover House for birthdays to be celebrated by everyone, regardless of age or how long they had been a resident. Just before Julie had arrived at the home 'Wee Willy' had enjoyed a birthday party like he'd never known before, and he was only expected to be there for a few weeks. The staff believed that everybody there was a member of one big, happy family, and occasions like birthdays and Christmas should be celebrated accordingly.

"Surprise!"

Clover House

Julie nearly fell down the last couple of steps. All the residents were stood facing her beneath a large banner that read,

Happy Birthday Julie.

"How did you know?" she asked, still trying to get over the shock.

"I might have had something to do with that," said Leo as he stepped forward out of the small gathering. Mr Jacobs smiled, if Leo hadn't have told everyone two days ago then he would have done. He had everybody's birthdays marked on his year planner on his office wall.

The group lined up to give Julie the presents that they had bought themselves, or in the case of those that weren't allowed to go shopping alone, had been bought for them to give.

It was then that she noticed that Tommy Bishop was missing, and then she recalled him boasting the day before that someone was coming to take him out for the day. In truth Julie was relieved she could imagine him trying to spoil the day.

Fat Mary was the first to step forward, her offering was a small box chocolates. They weren't wrapped and Julie could see that the seal had been broken. She wouldn't be at all surprised if when she opens them later there were one or two missing.

Clover House

The twins were next. Without saying a word they approached, smiled, and held out a package for Julie, she accepted it and returned their smile. She was slightly confused when she opened it to find a new pack of playing cards.

Fish came next. "Hope you like it," he said giving her the present he'd chosen himself. It was perfectly wrapped with a pink bow on top. "It wasn't expensive but the lady in the shop gift wrapped it for me." Inside was a small bottle of perfume.

"It's lovely," said Julie embarrassing him with a peck on the cheek.

James and Dave were next. "I'm sorry we didn't know that Fish was going to buy you perfume as well." James gave Fish a dismissive glance.

Opening the gift Julie said, "A lady can never have too much perfume."

Dave turned to James and said, "I told you that was the case."

Willy was next. He held out his present but was a little reluctant to let go. After some prompting by Mr Green Willy let go and Julie accepted it with a "Thank you."

"What is it?" asked Willy, this was obviously one of those occasions where the item had been bought on his behalf. Julie opened it to find a manicure set in a small leather case. She covered her hands quickly not wanting people to see that she

Clover House

bites her nails. She made a mental note to start growing them tomorrow.

Next up was Leo. First of all he gave her a birthday card. She opened it and was quite taken back at how soppy it was. A cuddly teddy bear was on the front, not what she expected at all. Inside it was printed with the words Happy Birthday, Leo had added his name and underneath that, 'Without you a home is just a house.' She quickly closed the card and smiled at him.

He then gave her the smallest gift she had received so far. She thanked him and started removing the gold foil that was the wrapping paper. "Is it a wedding ring?" shouted Fish. The whole group started laughing, that was except for Julie and Leo. Mr Jacobs was holding his breath and crossing his fingers. He knew Leo could be impulsive, but surely not that.

Casting the paper to one side Julie held up the gift box and opened it slowly. The silver necklace sparkled. "It's a St Christopher," said Leo, "he's the patron saint of travellers." Julie looked at the gift and then at Leo. "I know what you're thinking, that you hadn't planned on taking many trips," then added with a wink, "Trust me."

She gently took the necklace out of its box, placed the box on the telephone table, and put the necklace on. Leo helped her to fasten it. He then

Clover House

thrust his left cheek forward. "Where's mine then?" When she turned his head and planted a big kiss on his lips the crowd let out an immature snigger with a couple cheers thrown in.

"Okay, this is from the staff," said Mr Jacobs stepping forward and pulling Leo back away from Julie. He gave her an envelope, inside she found a voucher for £20 and a card signed by all the staff. "We never know what to buy so we leave it to the individual."

Julie looked across to where Miss Stevenson, Marge and Mr Green were standing. "Thank you, thank you everybody, this is the best birthday I can ever remember. Leo started singing the 'Happy Birthday' song and they all joined in.

When they had finished they all left the hall and went about their business, that was except for Mary who held back and leant over to whisper something to Julie, making sure she was out of earshot of the others she said, "There a piece of paper inside the box telling you what flavour each chocolate is. If there is any you don't like then I will have them." She made this sound like she was doing Julie a favour, then she disappeared to join the others.

"I heard that," said Leo.

"She means no harm," replied Julie then she changed the subject, "this was all such a surprise."

Clover House

"Wait until you see the special dinner that Marge cooks up on these occasions, she really pushes the boat out."

"I'm looking forward to it. I especially liked your gift Leo," she said toying with the necklace between her fingers.

When dinner came Julie wasn't disappointed, Leo was right when he said that Marge pushes the boat out. There was a huge Turkey placed in the centre of the table, this was accompanied with every kind of vegetable imaginable.

The meal was enjoyed by everyone and spirits were high. This was reflected in the banter and Fish certainly wasn't going to let his suggestion drop, about thinking her gift was going to be a marriage proposal from Leo. He got down on one knee next to the table, "Please Julie, be my wife." His imitation of Leo was spot on, especially the accent, everybody laughed including the staff.

"Okay, okay Fish that's enough," said Leo taking the jest in the manner that it was given. Fish returned to his chair.

All of a sudden the kitchen door flew open and in walked Marge carrying the most amazing Birthday cake Julie had ever seen. It was covered in white icing with a single candle on top and below that Julie's name written in pink. Everyone burst in to another rendition of 'Happy Birthday to you'.

Clover House

"Come on Julie, make a wish and blow out the candle," shouted Mary licking her lips. Julie hesitated for a few seconds, took a deep breath and blew the candle out in one go. Everybody applauded.

"What did you wish for?" asked Leo.

"If I tell you it won't come true, that's what they say," replied Julie.

Leo accepted this but went on, "go on then or are you going to keep it a secret?"

She looked puzzled then asked, "Go on what? I told you I wasn't going to tell you my wish."

"Not your wish, your age. How old are you?" he asked.

"Leo French, you should never ask a lady her age," she said, coyly. He didn't accept this as an answer. He wasn't going to be brushed off as easily as he was the wish. He continued to stare at her.

"Stare all you want, I'm not going to tell you my age. All I will say is I'm not as old as you Leo." He sniggered and decided that this was the only answer he was going to get.

Just as the festivities were drawing to a close in walked Tommy Bishop accompanied by another man they didn't recognise. "So what's happening here then?" he asked.

"Just sit down and have some cake Tommy," said the man with him as he nodded in the direction of Mr Jacobs.

Clover House

"Don't mind if I do." He sat down, reached across the table and plunged his hand into the cake, only withdrawing it when he had grabbed a handful. He then shoved as much as he could into his mouth in one go.

"Tommy, we do have a knife you could have used," said Mr Green. Leo was furious he stood up quickly to confront Tommy but Julie held his arm.

"Please don't Leo. He's only doing it to get a reaction from you," she said. He sat back down slowly but didn't take his eyes off Tommy.

Mr Jacobs broke the tension by suggesting that maybe it was time they all moved through to the lounge so that Marge could start clearing up. "We'll stay and help Marge," announced Julie whilst looking at Leo for confirmation. She knew it would be wiser to keep Leo and Tommy apart as long as possible or at least until Leo had calmed down.

Later that afternoon when Tommy had gone out and everything had settled down again, Leo was alone watching television whilst Julie was taking her medication upstairs. He glanced over at Fat Mary sat on the sofa, as he expected she was devouring a chocolate bar and reading. He turned his attention back to the television. Something made him turn back and look closer at the back of the magazine she was holding. He shuffled to the edge of his chair to get a closer look. To get even closer he dropped to

Clover House

his knees and moved forward until he was just a few feet away. Mary lowered the magazine and said, "What the hell are you doing?"

"Can I borrow your magazine for just a few seconds Mary?" Anybody walking into the room would be hard pressed to guess what was happening. Leo on his knees at Mary's feet, a pleading expression on his face. Mary, chocolate bar in one hand, magazine in the other her expression was one of bewilderment.

"I'll let you have it back, promise." Mary looked down at the magazine then back at Leo.

"You do realise it's a woman's magazine Leo, make-up, gossip etc?" He didn't reply he just remained at her feet with the look of an abandoned dog.

Mary stood up, dropped the magazine onto the sofa and said, "It's all yours. I've finished with it anyway." She left the room thinking he was more of a freak than she did before.

Leo snatched up the magazine and returned to his chair. The last thing he wanted was to be found reading a magazine like this so he did a quick glance around to make sure he was alone. Looking at the cover he shook his head, not understanding the pleasure people got from reading about celebrities lives. He turned the magazine over to look at the picture that caught his attention in the first place. It

Clover House

showed four skeletons playing instruments, very similar to the ones Julie had on her t-shirt. At the top of the page it said in bold type, dripping in blood,

The Living Zombies Tour Dates

As well as dates it listed the venues where the band was booked to appear. He ran his finger down the whole list, his lips moving as he read the places to himself. Once he had absorbed the list he started at the top again looking for the nearest place to Leeds. He came to the conclusion that Manchester would be the obvious choice, even though it was about forty miles away. The date they were due to appear in Manchester was just three days away. He had a lot to plan in a short time.

He had been so entranced in the magazine that he didn't see Miss Stevenson enter the room. "Everything okay, Leo?" she asked. Leo jumped. His reflex was to shove the magazine behind his back and sit up straight.

"Fine thanks," he said, looking as guilty as anything.

"How's your boil?" she asked smiling and secretly curious at what she had caught him doing.

"Oh that's a lot better thanks. Not completely gone but smaller and doesn't hurt anymore." Then

Clover House

he added, whilst stroking the inside of his thigh, "...and the other lump has gone as well."

"How are you getting on with Julie?" asked Miss Stevenson.

Leo thought this a funny question so hesitated before answering, "Just fine." He then realised what she was really asking was, has she told you she is dying? "She told me about her medical condition if that's what you mean."

Miss Stevenson smiled to acknowledge what had been unsaid between them. "It's good that she's found a friend here."

Leo smiled back and changed the subject. "If you were going to go to Manchester, how would you get there?"

The unusual question and swift change of subject caught Miss Stevenson off guard. "Err, train probably, I suppose." Then with a suspicious voice she added, "Why?"

"No reason, just wondered." Miss Stevenson knew better than to try and get any more details from Leo. She had come to the conclusion a long time ago that when it comes to Clover House it's sometimes better not to work out what the residents were thinking or planning. She stared at him for a few seconds trying to read his mind. He obviously wasn't going to elaborate so she smiled, shook her head and left the room. As she left Julie entered.

Clover House

"Julie," Leo shouted in an exaggerated whisper as he beckoned her over. "Come and see what I've found." He recovered the magazine from behind his back.

Julie turned and watched Miss Stevenson going up the stairs, taking them two at a time. She turned back round to face Leo. "You never did explain what you two had been up to that time I saw you coming out of the office fastening your trousers."

"You a little jealous Miss Sykes?" Leo asked teasing her.

"I don't care what you get up to or with whom." Leo could tell she was a bit miffed.

"Seriously, I needed to see her about a boil I had on my bum. She gave me some antibiotics and that's pretty well got rid of it." Leo leant on his side and pointed at the area in question.

"Gross," said Julie turning her nose up in disgust. Leo believed he also saw a look of relief hidden beneath the grimace.

"Forget that, come and sit down I have something to show you." Leo held up the magazine. Julie was curious. She sat next to him looking over at what he was holding. When he turned it over to the back page she instantly recognised the image.

"Oh my God it's 'The Living Zombies." Once again she was wearing the smile that warmed Leo's heart. He pointed to the tour dates further down the

Clover House

page. Julie looked closer to see what he was pointing at. Then it suddenly dawned on her. "No! No way!" she sat there with her mouth open. "We are going to Manchester to see them?"

"Ssshhh," Leo said putting his forefinger to his lips. "It's going to have to be a secret there is no way Mr Jacobs would ever let us go." Julie was nearly overcome with excitement. "It's in three days. It says it's an afternoon performance so we should be able to go and be back without anybody even knowing we were missing."

"I can't believe I'm going to actually see them." Julie was clapping her hands rapidly, a habit she had when excited.

"Well it is number two on your wish list," Leo said more than satisfied with himself.

Leo spent the rest of the afternoon researching everything he needed to know about their intended excursion. He checked on buses to the train station, trains to and from Manchester, how to get from the station to the venue. He left no stone unturned, he even downloaded maps that gave precise directions and distances. Once he had all the information he went through it all with a fine tooth comb.

The night before the concert they arranged to meet in the dining room after everyone else had left. "Is everything ready?" Julie asked already knowing the answer.

Clover House

Leo tapped the folder he held to his chest. "Don't you worry about anything, when Leo French takes a job on you can rely on it being done properly," he winked and tapped the folder again, "every detail is in here."

"Just a minute," said Julie, a thought had just occurred to her. "How the hell are we going to pay for all this, I don't have any money." A look of disappointment swept over her.

"Don't worry. Remember I said I saved half of my allowance and you asked what I was saving for?"

"Yes," she answered. "You said you'd know what you were saving for when the time came."

"Exactly, this is the time. I have a few hundred stashed away in my bedroom so don't worry. Call it a gift for all your birthdays I've missed." He wasn't sure if it was something he'd said but Julie's eyes had started to well up. "What's wrong?" he asked putting the folder down and taking her into his arms.

She pretended to hit him in the chest. "Nothing's wrong stupid, it's just that no one has ever been so kind to me before." She nestled back into him trying to hide her sobs.

Even though they had both wrapped up warm and it was the end of June, England could be a cold place to stand and wait for a bus.

Clover House

"It's ten minutes late," said Julie walking on the spot to try and warm her feet. Leo couldn't believe things weren't running to plan after all the work he'd put into preparing this trip. Just as he was going to console her the bus turned the corner. As it pulled up it went through a small puddle splashing Leo's freshly ironed jeans. Julie put her hands over her mouth and started blowing as if to warm them in truth she was trying to hide a smile.

"Two tickets to Bridge Street please," said Leo placing a five pound note in front of the driver. Without saying a word the driver hit the buttons on the machine and the tickets rolled out of the top. "Thanks." Leo picked up the tickets, accepted his change and followed Julie down the bus.

"How do you know where to get off?" asked Julie her eyes darting all over as if she'd never been on a bus before.

"Look, don't you worry about anything. Everything has been organised, you just enjoy the day." Julie sat back and began to look a little more relaxed. She even produced a packet of mints and offered Leo one. "Ah, I see I'm not the only who's come prepared." Julie smiled, linked her arm through Leo's and put her head on his shoulder.

About ten minutes into the journey Leo suddenly sat up right, knocking Julie's jaw with his shoulder. "I've just thought of something," he looked

Clover House

scared, "your medication, your injection?" Julie tried to calm him down, she went on to explain.

"It's okay. I can have my injection when we get back. As long as I have one every twenty-four hours and the tablets I have to take, I've brought with me." She pulled a small clear bottle from her pocket and began shaking the contents.

"That's okay then," said Leo, relief written all over his face.

Once they'd arrived at the train station it took them a while to work out exactly which train they needed. There had been a slight problem with Leo's preparations, apparently he'd been looking at an old timetable on-line, but a quick word with the man at the ticket booth and it had all been sorted out. He told them which platform to wait at and the fact it was running thirteen minutes late. Whilst Julie visited the toilet, Leo did a double check on his financial situation, not only was the timetable wrong but so were the prices. It had cost him a lot more than he'd budgeted for but he had brought extra for just such an occasion.

Arriving in Manchester both Leo and Julie were greeted by a crowd the size of which none of them had ever seen before. It was the day Manchester United played Chelsea. Everybody seemed to be wearing blue and the amount of policemen milling

Clover House

about warned Leo that this was a situation that could potentially get out of hand. As fast as possible Leo guided Julie through the crowds and out of the station. Holding her hand he pulled her into a small alley so he could check the paperwork in his folder.

"We need to get the number 9 bus, it's only a short journey but because of this crowd I'm thinking it may be easier just to jump into a taxi.

"Won't that be expensive?" Julie asked looking concerned.

"Don't worry I've got it covered." Leo was more worried about Julie getting knocked over by the crowd or getting hurt if a scuffle broke out. They walked about one hundred yards in the opposite direction to the one the football supporters were taking, and more by luck than good judgment came across a taxi rank. They jumped into the leading car and Leo told the driver the destination he wanted. The driver hesitated. "It's okay I have the money," said Leo.

"Are you sure that is where you want to go," asked the Asian driver.

"Yes please," replied Leo. He looked at Julie and she seemed as puzzled by the question as Leo was.

Fifteen minutes later. They were stood on a quiet street in the middle of a housing estate that looked like it had seen better days. As the taxi pulled

Clover House

away Leo looked around trying to get his bearings. What he saw didn't look like anything he'd seen on the street view on Google Earth. "Are we in the right place?" asked Julie. She too was looking around trying to imagine why anyone would hold a rock concert near this dump.

"The place is supposed to be here on Clarendon Street." Julie looked at the sign high up on the wall behind Leo, it read Clarence Street.

"Did you ask for Clarendon Street when we got into the taxi? Leo followed her gaze, looked up and saw the sign.

"Fuck!" he shouted at the top of his voice. "The dozy, deaf, twat!" Julie couldn't remember ever hearing Leo swear before so this sudden outburst scared her. "I wanted this day to be perfect and now it's ruined," he said as he kicked the bottom of a lamppost.

"No it's not. There's a shop over there we'll just ask the owner where we need to go." Without waiting for a response Julie marched over to the off-licence and went inside. A few minutes later she returned. Leo had calmed down and was looking a little crest fallen. "I'm sorry Julie, I just wanted it all to go like clockwork."

"The shop keeper said we're some distance from where we need to be. He said just follow this road right to the end, turn right and keep going." Leo

Clover House

knew there wasn't going to be any chance of getting a taxi around here and he had no idea when and where the buses went. The only thing they could do was walk.

An hour later and they arrived at the venue. It was a large open green area that had been fenced off for the occasion. Leo was aware that it wasn't just going to be The Living Zombies performing at the festival but he had no idea the kind of crowd that would be attending, there were thousands of people milling around. One area he could see had been designated for camping. Fortunately the weather had been good over the previous week so there wasn't the mud to contend with.

Leo looked across at Julie she hadn't said a word for the last twenty minutes. He could see a dark shadow under her eyes and as their walk had progressed she had become slower and slower. On one occasion he saw her discreetly taking one of the tablets from the bottle she'd shown him on the train, gulping it down without the aid of water. He hadn't dared ask how she is as he was well aware that this was one of her pet hates, people asking all the time.

At the entry gate they joined the line of people all pushing and shoving trying to get to the front. Checking his watch Leo realised that the time the band were due on stage had long passed. He was

Clover House

crossing his fingers that things were running late and that the whole trip hadn't been a waste of time.

"Have your tickets ready!" shouted a man at the fence where just behind him several colleagues were clipping them with a special machine.

Leo froze. Julie stopped, looked up at him and asked what the problem was. "It's the tickets," he replied clutching his folder to his chest.

"What do you mean it's the tickets? What's wrong with them?" She'd adopted her angry stance, legs apart arms folded.

"I... err... don't have any." Leo took a step back from her.

After what they had been through today he could see her lashing out at him, and deservedly so. It looked like it was to be a day punctuated with bad language. "What the fuck do you mean you have no tickets?" Leo could have sworn he'd actually seen her teeth grinding together.

Julie slumped down onto the grass. She hadn't blamed Leo for anything else that had gone wrong so far that day, but how in God's name can you forget the tickets. "Do you mean you left the tickets back at the home? Are you sure they're not in your folder? Have you checked?" Leo didn't even need to look. He already knew the tickets weren't in the folder, he even knew that they weren't back at Clover House. That was because he never bought any. He'd seen them on the web site but you had to have a bank account or credit card or something to order them. All he had was cash.

"Don't worry Julie, I'll sort it out." He went to the side of the queue where the man was shouting the warning to have your tickets ready. "Excuse me where can I buy a ticket?" Leo asked this not even knowing if he had brought enough money to buy some.

"You can't buy them here. You had to get them on-line and if you don't have one now then I'm sorry you can't come in. They sold out last night." Leo hesitated before turning back to face Julie, he could feel her eyes piercing his back.

"Did I hear you say you wanted some tickets?" Leo turned around to find a small scruffy man staring up at him, he stepped back slightly as the man's body odour hit him. "I've got a couple here I can let you have for thirty quid each." Leo didn't even need to check how much money he had left. He knew that after paying for the return train journey he couldn't afford them.

"No thanks." he said as he turned and started walking to where Julie was sat.

Julie could tell by the expression on Leo's face and the way he walked with his shoulders slumped that he hadn't had any luck. He dropped down beside her, lifted her hand and said, "I'm sorry. I wanted this day to be so special and I've gone and ruined it." Julie forced a smile. The long walk had taken its toll. She didn't say anything to Leo but she was starting to feel a little dizzy. At the moment she couldn't care less about seeing a band, all she wanted was to go home and lay down.

They sat together for about fifteen minutes. In the distance they could hear a woman singing or screeching, depending on your taste in music. The crowd was cheering and singing along with her. "I think I may struggle to walk back to the train station," said Julie. After the rest she'd had and the tablet she'd taken when walking here she was starting to feel better, but she'd said this hoping Leo would take the hint and pay for a taxi back.

Leo was staring at something over her shoulder. "I have an idea. You may not even have to walk to the taxi." He jumped up and strolled past Julie towards a large tent with a red cross on the top. She watched as he nonchalantly circled the tent with his hands in his pockets kicking the odd tuft of grass as he went.

After he'd circled the tent three times he went back behind it again and out of sight, this time it seemed to take ages before he re-emerged. When he did he wasn't alone. From somewhere he had commandeered a wheelchair and was now pushing it back down the hill towards Julie. Though his head

Clover House

was bent low she could see the grin he was wearing. When he saw her looking he gave her a sly wink.

"Your carriage awaits madam," he said in a posh voice as he pulled up alongside her.

"I'm not getting in that," she said. As she tried to stand her left leg gave away slightly and Leo had to catch her.

He continued using the posh voice "I think you are madam. I have just risked my freedom and probably a custodial sentence to obtain this for you." Julie smiled and lowered herself into the chair. Leo looked around for the best way to exit in a stolen wheelchair. He saw a path that ran alongside the makeshift fence that surrounded the festival. Getting to the path over the uneven ground was the hard part but once there the ride was relatively smooth. He pushed her gently down the hill and, because of the gradient he didn't have to use much effort, in fact he was able to lean on the handles and take the weight off his bad leg. His leg had been hurting all day and the long walk had done it no good at all.

"Come along, come along," a jolly voice said behind them. Leo turned to find a man pushing a wheelchair followed by about twenty others. Leo moved to one side to let them past, they were obviously in a hurry. The man looked Leo up and down then his eyes did the same to Julie. He looked back at Leo and said, "You should be wearing your

Clover House

pass. Never mind now, keep up." Just ahead a gate in the fence had opened up. Just to the left of the gate a sign read,

PRIVATE
Performers and disabled access
Please keep clear

A couple of the other wheelchairs had passed Leo so now they were in the middle of the line. Julie twisted in the chair and looked up at Leo. "We can't... can we?"

"We certainly can," replied Leo, getting as close to the chair ahead as he could. As they passed the security guard Leo could see him glancing down at the passes the people pushing the chairs were wearing around their necks. As Leo drew level with the guard he turned his back to him and shouted at the rest of the chairs behind "Come on keep up at the back." As he passed the guard he turned again and continued pushing Julie. They went down a gravel path that ran behind the stage. As they turned the corner the first thing to hit Julie was the noise, everybody was screaming and waving their arms. She was pushed towards the crowd that were being held back by a barrier that was obviously built for the job. Almost in unison all the chairs were turned 180 degrees. Walking on to the stage in full costume were The Living Zombies.

Clover House

For the next two hours Julie joined the rest of the crowd singing along, screaming, and waving her arms. Leo didn't really appreciate the band or their music, he was content to just stand and watch Julie's face light up as they began each song. Whilst Julie was watching the band Leo leant over the barrier and tapped the shoulder of a man selling memorabilia, a minute later he was wrapping a scarf around Julie's neck that was printed to match her 'Living Zombies' t-shirt. She said something he couldn't hear so he bent down closer. She mouthed the words 'thank you' grabbed the lapels of his jacket and pulled him closer so she could kiss him. As they separated she said something else that Leo couldn't quite make out. It seemed very much like 'I love you'.

The man who had been leading the wheelchairs nudged Leo and said, "Steady on old boy, we're supposed to just push them around." Leo apologised.

As the last song came to an end, Julie was reflecting on what an incredible day she'd had. The crowd shouted for an encore and Julie joined in. The lead singer raised his hand up and down to quieten the crowd. Eventually you could hear a pin drop.

The band leader said, "We have one more song to sing." The crowd went crazy. Then at his request they went silent once again. "It's for a very special person and it's a little different to what you guys are used to hearing us play." He turned, nodded to his bass player and began singing the sweetest song Julie had ever heard. He walked to the side of the stage and slowly descended the wooden stairs. He continued singing as he walked straight over to Julie and knelt in front of her wheelchair. He held her hand, winked at Leo, and sang every word straight into her eyes. If Julie had died that afternoon she would have died the happiest person in the world.

Clover House
Chapter 8

Leaving the festival Julie just couldn't stop talking about it. She was reliving every moment. "I can't believe he actually came down and sang to me. Out of all those thousands of people he chose me." She gripped the wheels of the wheelchair stopping it dead. Turning round slowly she said to Leo, "You had something to do with it, didn't you?"

He lifted both hands in the air as if surrendering. "I confess. While you were watching the band I needed the toilet so I went behind the stage looking for it. Even though it was only for the performers and the roadies there was still quite a queue. I ended up talking to a guy that was working with 'The Living Zombies' so I jotted some details on a scrap of paper and asked him to pass it on."

She smiled and turned back to face the front. "I suppose I can let you off this time Leo French, but don't you go sneaking off doing things behind my back again.

Julie didn't know if it was the rest she'd had sitting down, the tablet or just the adrenaline pouring through her body that made her feel so much better. After waiting at the bus stop for twenty-five minutes it finally arrived. On lookers were astounded when Julie just got up out of the wheelchair and climbed aboard the bus. "Wow it's a

Clover House

miracle," said Leo to the people watching. They did feel rather bad about just abandoning the chair but whilst waiting for the bus they agreed there wasn't any other option.

The bus arrived in the city centre. As they stepped off Leo checked his watch, it was already 7:30pm. Mr Jacobs didn't have a curfew at Clover House but if you were going to be back later than 8pm then you were supposed to let the member of staff on duty know why.

After asking a passer-by directions to the train station Leo asked Julie if she would be okay walking the 300 yards yet to travel. "I'm fine," she said. And to be honest, Leo had never seen her looking so radiant. "I just don't want today to end. It's been the best day of my life," she added.

"Then let's make it last just a little longer." Leo grabbed Julie's hand and almost dragged her across the road. A taxi had to break hard to avoid hitting them, the driver hanging out of the window shouting expletives at them both.

"Leo, where are we going?" Julie was confused.

"Here." They were stood at the foot of some stone steps. Julie followed Leo's pointing finger to the top, it looked like the entrance to some kind of night club or high class bar.

"They won't let us in there," said Julie as if the idea was completely ridiculous.

Clover House

"Why not? Our money is as good as anyone else's." Still holding her hand Leo escorted her up the steps. Greeting them at the top were two very large bouncers in dinner suits. They hesitated for a while then Leo squeezed Julie's hand and stepped towards the door. The two bouncers closed the gap between them with a single side step, blocking their entrance. Leo took a step back so he could look up into their faces. "Is there a problem gentlemen?" asked Leo.

The bouncers smiled at each other, then the taller one said. "You could say that. I think it may be better for you to try somewhere else tonight...Sir."

"Come on Leo, let's just go and get the train," said Julie trying to pull Leo away.

Leo ignored her and took a step closer to the one that had just spoken. "Is it a colour thing?" Leo said rubbing the side of his face.

The two bouncers looked at each other and smiled. "No it's an age thing," the bouncer replied hoping he would take his girlfriend's advice and leave. Leo looked at the sign above the door that stated you had to be above twenty-one years old to enter and that entrance was at the digression of the management.

"We are over twenty-one," said Leo.

The two bouncers burst out laughing. At that point the door behind them opened and a man in a

Clover House

shirt and tie stepped out. He was wearing a badge that read Manager. "What's going on, Carl?"

Again the taller bouncer, who seemed the more vocal of the two, said, "This gentleman and his lady friend want to come in, I suggested they try somewhere else.

The Manager looked Leo and Julie up and down and said, "What the hell. It's early and we're nearly empty. Let them in." Leo gave the two bouncers the smuggest look he could muster as he followed the Manager in to the building.

Inside, the bar area was decorated in gold and silver. Strategically positioned lights reflected of the surfaces spraying the room with stars. Julie just stood with her mouth open. She'd never seen anything like it. The first thing that came to Leo's mind was he'd made a mistake. Drinks in this place were going to cost a fortune. "What would you like to drink?" he asked Julie.

As if she was reading his mind she said, "I'll just have a coke please. Can you make it diet?" He sauntered up to the bar where a young lady was drying a glass, just for something to do.

"Can I have two diet cokes please?"

Without saying a word she pulled two glasses from under the bar, reached down again and lifted two bottles of diet coke from a fridge. She opened

Clover House

them and poured them out. "That will be £4.60 please."

Leo thought he'd misheard her. "Pardon?"

"Two diet cokes. That will be £4.60." Leo rummaged in his pocket and eventually pulled out the exact amount in change. When he turned around he saw that Julie had seated herself at a table in the corner. He carried the drinks across and joined her.

"How much were they?" she asked almost cringing awaiting the answer.

"Don't you worry about that," but Leo was worrying. His money was all but gone.

Music started blasting out of the speakers. Then suddenly it was brought back down to a reasonable level. "Thank God for that," said Leo. "After being in front of the speakers on that stage all day I don't think my ears could take much more."

"Leo French, don't tell me you're getting old before your time?" Julie laughed out loud and this caught the attention of the few other people that were in the bar. Leo saw the Manager that had given them permission to come in, stop his conversation with two girls and stare at them.

Anybody watching would guess that neither of them seemed to be enjoying themselves, they just sat not daring to talk and taking the odd sip from they're drinks. Julie stood up and held out her hand.

Clover House

"Fancy a dance?" Opposite the bar there was a small dance floor with a DJ's booth overlooking it.

Leo glanced in that direction. "There's no one else dancing," he said looking at Julie's outstretched hand as if it was something to avoid at all cost.

"Somebody has to be the first up." She stood her ground.

"I can't dance," Leo said glancing around the room to see if anybody was watching.

"Everybody can dance. It's just that some people are better at it than others. I don't care how good you are." She wasn't going to take no for an answer. As she reached for Leo's hand he pulled it away.

"It's my leg. I've been on it all day and it's feeling rather sore." He rubbed his thigh and grimaced.

"Then I'll be gentle," she said sarcastically. Julie grabbed his wrist and with all her strength she pulled Leo to his feet and escorted him the short distance to the dance floor. Once there she turned around, put her arms around his neck and started swaying side to side in time to the music. Not knowing what else to do Leo put his hands on her hips and leaned side to side. "I know you have a bad leg but you're dancing like you are paralyzed from the waist down. Move your hips not your shoulders." She pulled him closer so he didn't have any other choice than to sway as

Clover House

she was doing. She snuggled her nose under his ear and started humming the words to the song.

They must have been on the dance floor for nearly an hour. Leo felt like he'd been under a trance for the whole time. He was brought out of it when he bumped into someone else. He hadn't even realised anybody else had joined them. He looked down at his watch. "Oh my God, Julie, have you seen the time? "Julie glanced down at her watch but didn't seem as alarmed as Leo.

"It's 8.30. We need to find a phone before they start sending out the search party." They hurried back to their table and downed the cokes in one. Julie pulled a face as it had gone a bit flat.

They raced out of the building, past the bouncers and down the steps. Leo glanced around and saw a phone booth on the other side of the road. "Wait here." He ran across the road opened the booth's door and reached for the handset. There was nothing there, just a dangling piece of cable. "Shit!" he shouted as he kicked one of the small windows. Outside he waved his hand to beckon Julie over.

Unlike Leo she looked both ways, waited for a bus to pass then walked across. "What's the problem?" She could tell there was one just by the look on his face.

Clover House

"The phone's knackered. Let's go down this street and try and find another one." They walked up and down street after street for the next fifteen minutes until eventually they found one. Julie waited outside while Leo called Clover House. He picked up the receiver and sighed with relief when he heard a dialling tone. Sliding his hand into his jeans pocket he held his breath, praying he had some change. His emotions were mixed as he looked at the contents. He had plenty of change but that was all. He didn't have enough for the fare home. "I'll deal with that later." He mumbled to himself as he watched Julie through the small scratched window trying to keep herself warm.

"Hello," said Leo in a confident voice.

"Is that you Leo? Where are you?" Leo recognised Mr Green's voice, "are you on your way back?" he added.

"Yes Mr Green. It's Leo. I'm with Julie Sykes but our bus from town has broken down so we maybe a while yet. I just didn't want you worrying about us." Leo winked at Julie and gave her a 'thumbs-up' sign through the window, she smiled back. It would have been a completely different ball game if Mr Jacobs had answered, he wouldn't have been as easy to convince. "I'm not sure what time we will be back but it will be as soon as we can." He picked up a piece of newspaper from the shelf and started rustling it into the mouth piece. "Sorry Mr Green, you're breaking up." Leo hung up the phone before Mr Green had time to say anything.

"What did they say?" Julie asked.

"Mr Green is on duty tonight so I just explained that the bus from town had broken down and we'd get back as soon as possible." As he was speaking Leo was glancing up and down the street trying to get his bearings. Whilst looking for a phone they had taken so many turns he was completely lost.

"We are lost aren't we?" He was now even more convinced that Julie could read minds. He had a vision of them appearing on a television show him in the audience holding up a watch and Julie on a stage blindfolded announcing, "It's a Rolex watch and its four minutes slow," he smiled to himself.

"What's so funny?" she asked as she too was looking up and down for a clue as to where they were.

"Nothing, I think it's this way," Leo said as he marched off in the opposite direction to the one Julie was just about to suggest. He turned to see she wasn't making any effort to increase her speed to catch up so he stopped and waited for her, "are you alright?" Even in the decreasing light Leo could see that she wasn't. Her features had started to take on the same appearance as when she had started to feel ill earlier in the day.

Clover House

"I should really have had my injection by now," she replied as she stopped walking completely and leant against the wall.

"What about the pills, can't you just take another one of those? They seemed to do the trick last time." Leo was starting to panic. They were in the middle of nowhere, miles from her medication at Clover House and no means to get there.

"What do we have here?" said one of the five men that came around the corner. All of them had shaved heads and leather jackets on as though it was some kind of uniform. Leo turned his back to them hoping they would just walk by, no such luck.

"Don't turn your back on me," said the one that had spoken, spinning Leo round by the shoulder to face him. "It's rude to ignore someone when they ask you a question." He looked back at his friends and on cue they all sniggered.

"Look I don't want any trouble, me and my girlfriend just got lost." Without realizing it he and Julie were now surrounded by the gang. He waited for a reply from any of them but there was none coming. He grabbed Julie's hand and started to move towards a gap that had opened up between them. They closed the gap. "Okay what do you guys want? We don't have any money." Leo turned his pockets inside out to show them.

Clover House

The one that Leo had presumed was the leader, because he did all the talking moved towards Julie. He grabbed both ends of the Living Zombie's scarf Leo had bought earlier and gave it a tug, as she fell towards him she gave out a little yelp. Leo rushed forward but two of the gang members held him back, he tried to wrestle free but they were too big. "So what do you see in him?" asked the leader, then he added, "he's black." This was something that had never even crossed Julie's mind before but the fact this moron thought that it could ever be an issue infuriated her.

She was only inches from her captive's face. Smiling she said, "Well you know what they say about black men." At the same time she rammed her knee right up into his groin. The way it winded him you would have thought she'd hit him in the stomach. He let go of the scarf, closed his eyes and crumpled to the floor at her feet. Leo looked around for a response from the other gang members. It looked like they were just trying to mask their smiles.

The police car pulled up alongside them without anybody having time to run. Its front wheels mounted the curb to block an exit one way and the two policemen inside ran around the back to prevent anybody making off in that direction. As they approached Leo, Julie and the gang one of the

Clover House

officers spoke into the radio clipped to his lapels, he was asking for a van and back-up.

"So what's going on here then?" asked the one, with baton in one hand and his pepper spray canister in the other. Leo could see why he was being so defensive, they were outnumbered. Julie started to explain but was stopped before she could get a word out. "You keep quiet," she was told by one of the officers. "It was you we saw doing the assaulting as we turned the corner. You can have your say down at the station."

Leo stepped forward. "You can't do that officer she needs her medication, we have to go."

"Nobody is going anywhere tonight," said the policeman with the baton, waving it in Leo's face. "You two stand over there." Leo and Julie were physically dragged to the side of the wall near the front of the car.

By now the gang member on the floor was beginning to get his breath back. He rose slowly, swearing at the police officers. This seemed to muster the rest of the gang as all the others started goading the officers also; they were all looking for a fight. The policeman that requested back-up earlier shouted his request again into the radio. Slightly panicked his colleague sprayed his pepper spray into the face of the gang leader as he came too close.

Clover House

It may have been inexperience or just bad luck but the officer doing the spraying hadn't taken into consideration the evening breeze, the result of which meant most of the spray went into his and his partners face. As they spluttered and coughed the gang ran past them and down the road, the leader slightly behind limping a little.

Leo looked around and like the others decided to take the opportunity. He ran around the front of the police car, opened the driver's door and jumped in. He reached across the seat and flicked the switch that opened the passenger's side. As the door hit Julie in the back it jolted her to her senses, up to that point she was trying to work out what was happening. She heard Leo scream, "Get in." Without another thought she jumped into the police car and closed the door.

"Hang on. What the hell do you think you're doing? You can't steal a police car. In fact, come to that, do you even know how to drive a car?" Before she had a chance to open the door and get out, Leo had rammed the gear stick into reverse, gunned the throttle and skidded away, leaving the two policemen squinting and rubbing their eyes to try and see what was happening.

As they drove down the road, Leo toyed with the different switches trying to turn off the flashing blue lights. "Ah that's it," he said as the lights

Clover House

stopped. "In answer to your question I have been playing 'Grand Theft Auto' for years."

Julie stared at him. "You mean you have never driven a real car before?" The sound of grinding gears made her turn in her seat and fasten the safety belt. Leo did likewise.

"What do you think, but I'm not doing too badly am I?" Before she could answer he added, "anyway, we need to get you back for your medication and this looks to me like the fastest way to do it." Julie conceded he did have a point, but she could also see by the expression on his face that he was quite enjoying himself. He nodded his head towards a sign they were passing, it read 'Leeds 47miles'.

"By the way, what do they say about black men?" Leo asked.

Julie knew he was teasing so she smiled back at him and said, "Little brains."

It took them quite a while to find the M62 motorway back to Leeds, during this time Leo had managed to gain control of the car. Leo had also remembered seeing this motorway on one of his maps when he did his research, little did he know then that he'd be using it to drive back... in a police car.

Clover House

The motorway had been relatively clear, that was until they approached the Huddersfield turn-off. In the distance Leo could see the red glow from all the brake lights from the stationary traffic, there must have been an accident.

He slowed the vehicle right down and joined the waiting traffic. "I have an idea." His eyes scanned along the buttons on the dashboard. He flicked the one marked 'Blues' then did the same to the one marked '2/tones'. Immediately the flashing blue lights and the siren started. The traffic ahead started to part, each car moving to the side leaving a gap down the centre.

"Leo you can't," said Julie as she covered her face from the passengers they passed.

"Oh but I can," replied Leo who was obviously getting pleasure out of the experience, he even waved to thank those that moved out of his way.

As they neared the accident Leo could see a number of emergency vehicles at the site, they too had the blue lights flashing. As he drew alongside them he pulled down his sun visor to create a shadow on his face. He waved to one of the officers taking down details in his black book and sped off. If the other officers at the crash site had been in their vehicles ten minutes ago they would have heard the 'All-points' bulletin from despatch telling them to look out for Leo's stolen police car.

Clover House
Chapter 9

Leo looked out of his bedroom window at the police car that was parked just down the road. When they had arrived back last night they had entered to find Mr Green asleep in front of the television. Leo wrote a note and left it on his chest. It read simply, 'Back home didn't want to disturb you.' He had then taken Julie up to her bedroom and made sure she administered her injection and that she was safely tucked up in bed. He felt quite pleased with himself at how the night had ended. The fact that he didn't have the train fare home could have been a major hiccup.

He suddenly remembered how last night he'd fished out some change and put it into the public phone. He dashed over to the change spread on his bedside table and started rummaging through the coins. There it was. He held up the lucky 50p piece Julie had found and given him. As he looked at the engraving of the airmen he said out loud, "maybe you are a lucky talisman after all."

As he sat on the window sill he watched another police car pull up behind the one he had parked last night. He hadn't wanted to park it so close to the home but Julie was in no condition to walk anywhere. Two policemen got out, one made

Clover House

straight for Clover House the other stopped awhile to look inside the police car he'd abandoned. The policeman scratched his chin when he saw the 'Manchester Police' logo on the side, but then seemed to dismiss it and went to join his colleague.

Leo sat for the next ten minutes rehearsing his explanation as to why he stole a police car. No matter how he phrased it in his head it seemed a feeble excuse when he said it out loud. Eventually the inevitable knock came to his door. He practised his surprised smile once more then went to see who it was. "Quick let me in and close the door," said Julie as she pushed past him. She sat on his bed twiddling her fingers and looking very guilty. "Have you seen who just arrived? I was watching television and when I turned around there they were. I nearly died." Bad choice of words Leo thought.

"Look, when we tell them what happened last night they will understand." Leo didn't even believe his own voice but tried to calm Julie. "We need to get our story straight. For a start I'll take all the blame, and look at it this way," Julie looked up and smiled waiting for the silver lining, "we completed number two on the wish list." It wasn't much as far as silver linings go, but the thought of yesterday kept the smile on Julie's face.

The knock, though expected, made them both jump. Leo rose from the bed where he'd been sat

Clover House

next to Julie. "Well this is it." He sounded like a condemned man going to the gallows. He walked over to the door, brushed himself down and put a smile on his face. The last person he was expecting to be stood there was Miss Stevenson.

She was wearing a solemn look and her head was bowed a little. "Leo, there's someone here to see you." She stepped to one side and let him go first. She smiled at Julie, nodded and closed the door behind her.

Miss Stevenson escorted Leo all the way to Mr Jacobs's office. As he walked through the house all the other residents were staring and wearing glum faces, that is except for Tommy Bishop who had a knowing smirk on his face. As Leo walked past him he ran his forefinger across his throat.

"Come in Leo take a seat," said Mr Jacobs, the two policemen he'd seen entering the building were stood to one side. Leo walked to the seat opposite Mr Jacobs's desk pulled it out and slumped into it.

"I can explain, you see...,"

Mr Jacobs started talking over Leo. "These gentlemen have brought some bad news. I'm sorry Leo."

"As I was saying I can explain everything. You see I took Julie to...," One of the police officers starting talking over Leo just as Mr Jacobs had.

Clover House

"I have some bad news Mr French." He coughed into his hand. "It's your mother. She was found this morning by one of her neighbours." He hesitated and looked at his colleague. "She was found dead."

It was a few seconds before Leo registered what had just been said. He had a thousand questions but they all seemed to be jumbled into one in his head. Subconsciously he started asking one but then jumped to another. "Why...where... I mean what?"

Mr Jacobs lifted himself from his chair and walked to Leo's side of the desk. He placed his hand on Leo's shoulder and started offering some kind of an apology, as if it had been his fault. "I'm sorry Leo. We all are. Of course we will help you with all the arrangements and anything else you need." He turned to face the policemen. "Thank you very much officers. I'll take it from here." He shook hands with them both as they left, both appeared eager to leave.

In a daze and without saying anything Leo stood up and walked out of the office, across the hall and straight out of the front door. Julie had been watching the office door at a safe distance, waiting for Leo to emerge handcuffed between the two policemen. She'd been relieved when she watched them leave without him, but now she was confused.

Clover House

She caught the door just before it closed and ran out after him. She didn't have to go far. Leo was sat on the grass near the gate crying. He was picking handfuls of clover and ripping them apart.

"Leo, whatever is the matter?" She sat down beside him rubbing his back with the palm of her hand.

It took him a while to answer but eventually he put down the shredded clover, and between sobs he said, "It's my mother. She's dead." Julie put both hands to her mouth with shock. This was the last thing she expected.

"How?" she asked. It was then that Leo realized he had walked out of the office without getting one answer to the thousands of questions that swam around his head.

"I don't know," he replied. Like a tape machine he rewound what he could remember of what they had been telling him, "something about, one of the neighbours finding her."

"I'm so sorry, Leo."

Leo wiped his eyes and looked up at her. "Why do people always do that, apologise as if it was their fault?" He grabbed another clump of clover from the grass.

"I think they're saying sorry for your loss." Julie put her arm around his shoulder and pulled him a bit

Clover House

closer for comfort. "You never really spoke about your mother. Were you close?"

"If we had been that close she wouldn't have put me in here." His voice was bitter. "I haven't seen her for two years." This confused Julie. If he hadn't been that close to her and hadn't seen her for two years he seemed awfully upset. It was Leo's turn to read Julie's mind. "The reason I'm upset is that I always imagined her turning up one day and taking me away from here. I suppose I know it was only a pipe dream, and that she'd never give up her booze to look after me.

He picked a single four leaf clover and held it up. "Looks like I'm going to be staying in this shit hole for the foreseeable future, so much for good luck." Julie picked the clover from between his fingers.

"I'm here," she said as she planted a kiss on his cheek. Leo smiled, but what was actually going through his mind was, yes, but for how long.

Over the next few days Leo and Julie didn't spend much time together. Leo didn't feel like company so he slipped back into his old routine of helping Marge in the kitchen and watching television. Julie accepted this and gave him the space he needed.

It was at breakfast one morning when Mr Jacobs entered the dining room with yet another

Clover House

newcomer. All the residents were half way through their breakfast so didn't appreciate having to go through the welcome ceremony. As instructed they put down their eating utensils and started the slow hand clap, which of course was supposed to be applause. "Thank you everybody. This is Charlie." everybody's eyes switched from Mr Jacobs to the puny little person next to him clutching a suitcase. He bowed, which made everyone laugh.

"Leo will you do the usual and take Charlie under your wing for the next couple of days." Leo said nothing but his face was pleading to be excused from this task.

Julie squeezed his hand under the table and whispered, "Say yes, for me." Leo hesitated then gave a nod in the direction of Mr Jacobs. Julie smiled and said, "I think it will do you good, a distraction." Charlie smiled at Leo.

Whilst Leo had been clearing away all the breakfast things he had been having second thoughts about being the newcomer's chaperone. He had decided to go and see Mr Jacobs and ask to be excused, he even thought about putting Julie's name forward as a replacement. Walking towards the Manager's office he noticed the door was shut, this was unusual as Mr Jacobs's motto was 'my door is always open'. As he got closer he could hear voices, there was obviously Mr Jacobs's but it took Leo a

Clover House

moment or two to recognise the other. Then it dawned on him, Mrs Westland.

He was about to leave them to it when he heard his name mentioned. He looked around to see if anybody was watching. There was nobody about so he placed his ear flat against the door.

"I hope you don't expect the Council to pay for his mother's funeral." Leo's eyebrows dipped.

"Well, she was living in a Council house and as far as I know she didn't have a penny to her name," said Mr Jacobs

"It's not our department and I thought you may bring this up so I've done some homework." He could hear her rustling some papers. "Here it is 'A Pauper's funeral'," she continued, obviously reading. "Under Section 46 of the Public Health Act 1984, in brackets Control of Disease, it states that if family members cannot pay for a funeral then the state must. Of course it will be done on the cheap."

Leo couldn't believe his ears. He knew Mrs Westland was a cow but how could she be so callous? He was just about to barge into the office when Mr Jacobs starting defending him, "I don't think any of that will be necessary."

"Oh, you have a secret stash for just such an occasion?" she asked sarcastically.

"No. Leo French has a little put away." Leo thought about his savings hidden in his bedroom, there was no way Mr Jacobs could know about that and after the Manchester trip there certainly wasn't enough to pay for a funeral.

"What do you mean, how much?" Leo could imagine Mrs Westland's eye's lighting up at the sound of money.

"I think it's about seven thousand pounds." Leo was dumb struck. How come nobody had ever told him about it? "Of course once he was sent here a 'Permanent Agent' had to be chosen to carry out his financial transactions." He could hear Mr Jacobs move away from his desk, then a filing cabinet drawer being pulled open. "Yes, here it is, almost seven and a half thousand pounds." He listened as the cabinet drawer was pushed closed then a desk drawer open and shut.

Leo was on one hand relieved that his mother wouldn't have to go through a pauper's funeral but he was annoyed that they were keeping his money from him.

"Well at least that's sorted then. Will you be taking care of arrangements Mr Jacobs?" asked Mrs Westland.

"What are you doing? Who are you listening to?" Leo spun round to find the new resident, Charlie, stood right behind him. "Are you listening in on other people's conversations?"

Clover House

"No." Leo dropped to his knees. "I was just looking for something I dropped around here somewhere. The door to the Manager's office opened and Mrs Westland stepped out and nearly fell over Leo.

"What on earth, get out of my way you stupid person." She pushed past Leo and knocked Charlie sideways as she went past him.

"Is there something I can help you with Leo?" asked Mr Jacobs.

Leo stood up quickly but before he could reply Charlie stepped forward and said, "Mr Jacobs I found Leo list.....,"

Leo stood between them and finished his sentence for him. "My new friend Charlie is going around telling everybody how he loves it when I...list all the things down for him, rules, eating times etc."

Mr Jacobs looked dubiously at Leo. "Okay Leo, keep up the good work." Leo had got out of that situation but he was now stuck with this little grass.

The funeral was to be next Friday, that was exactly two weeks from when his mother had died. Leo couldn't understand it, he had seen lots of programmes, when people die in other countries and other religions, and they are buried virtually the same day. He put it down to the country "going to the dogs", to quote somebody on 'Question Time'

Clover House

last night. He didn't really have any input with regards the organisation of the funeral, but he didn't mind.

He was also coming to terms with the situation with the help of Julie. They had started spending more and more time together over the last week and were now almost inseparable again. The only problem they had, was Charlie, he tried to follow them everywhere. Leo thought he must be a bit slow in the head not to take the hint that he didn't want anything to do with him, especially after what happened outside Mr Jacobs's office.

The arcade became their sanctuary. Nobody else at the home knew about it so quite often they would sneak out the back and meet there. Julie was getting better at Leo's favourite game though she would be the first to admit she never expected to beat him. He was a natural.

After one such trip to the arcade they returned to Clover House so Julie could take her injection and Leo could help Marge prepare the evening meal. She ran up the stairs to her bedroom after blowing him a kiss, he continued walking towards the kitchen. Leo suddenly fell forward after receiving a sharp push in the back. He only maintained his balance by grabbing the back of a chair. When he turned around he saw Tommy Bishop in the door way. He copied Julie and blew Leo a kiss. "There you go lover boy." He

Clover House

pretended to make himself sick by pushing two fingers down his throat.

"Just let me go Tommy I don't want any trouble." Leo glanced around, they were on their own.

"Well maybe I do." Tommy stepped forward, puffing his chest out, "and what's this I hear about you being a poor little orphan now?"

Leo ground his back teeth together. "Let's not do this Tommy."

"Come on little black boy, I'll give you the first punch for free." Leo knew that Tommy was nearly twice his size and weight. In a fight he wouldn't stand a chance.

"Tommy just let me walk away and nobody gets hurt."

"By nobody I assume that means you." Tommy was moving slowly closer. Out of the corner of Leo's eyes he could see him screwing his fists up ready to attack. Remembering how Julie dealt with the thug in Manchester Leo decided to try the same thing. As soon as Tommy was in reach Leo swung his leg back, but instead of hitting him with his knee he let him have the full force of his boot.

Nothing!

Tommy didn't even flinch. "So, you made the first move then, I think that gives me the right to retaliate." Tommy moved forward engulfing Leo like

Clover House

a tidal wave. The first punch caught Leo under the chin crunching his teeth together. As his head went back another struck him right in the stomach, making him double over. His head went down and Tommy's knee came up to meet it. That was the last thing Leo remembered of that day.

After giving herself the injection Julie put her medication away and started making her way down the stairs. She made it about half way before a grunting noise made her stop. It sounded like someone doing hard exercise. She decided to check it out. Following the sound she went across the hall, through the lounge and into the dining room. She could hear the noise coming from behind the table, she crept forward. At first all she could see was Tommy Bishop's back, then she saw a pair of legs sticking out behind him, Leo's legs. It took her mind a few seconds to register what she was looking at. Then she saw Tommy raise one of his hands and bring it down in front of him accompanied by the grunt she'd heard on the stairs. She took another step forward, what she saw then made her feel physically sick. He was sat on Leo's chest pounding what was left of his face with his fists, blood was splattered everywhere. Without any kind of warning she grabbed a cricket bat that had been left leaning absently against the wall, brought it up to shoulder height, swung it behind her head and then back all

Clover House

the way around until it smacked Tommy right in the side of the head. Anybody downstairs at Clover House would have heard his skull split. Julie fell to her knees and began screaming.

Mr Jacobs ran into the room faster than he'd ever moved before. In front of him he found two bodies, both leaking blood profusely and to one side Julie crouched down crying, a cricket bat laid beside her. "What on earth have you done Julie?" he said more to himself than her. Mr Jacobs knew First Aid but this was beyond that. He pulled his mobile from his pocket and called the emergency services, requesting both ambulance and police. After giving the details he ended the call and without saying a word he sat down beside Julie and cautiously slid the cricket bat out of her reach.

"I had to, I had to. He was killing him." Mr Jacobs thought it inconceivable that Julie would do this to anybody let alone two people, but with that short sentence everything became clear. She had obviously had to hit Tommy to stop him attacking Leo. Mr Jacobs knew that Tommy was a bully with a very short temper and he'd had to reprimand him on several occasions, but he didn't see this coming.

It was probably only minutes but it seemed like hours before anybody else turned up. During that time Mr Jacobs had tried to stem the flow of blood from all the injuries as well as trying to placate Julie.

Clover House

A few of the residents had come in to see what all the commotion was and they took little notice as Mr Jacobs instructed them to wait outside. Mr Green had to usher them into the TV lounge.

The paramedics arrived at the same time as the police. As soon as Mr Jacobs saw them he stood up and stepped back to give them the room they needed to work.

The police cleared the room and escorted a hysterical Julie and Mr Jacobs into his office. They all sat down just as Marge entered carrying four cups of tea, she had missed the main show because she was late for work. One of the policemen removed his hat, took out a notebook and said to Mr Jacobs, "can you tell me what happened, starting at the beginning?"

It took a while for the policemen to get the full story, partly due to Julie being so upset and partly due to Mr Jacobs being distracted by the blood that covered his suit. He was constantly rubbing his hands together under the desk. Julie caught a glimpse of the paramedics carrying Leo out on a stretcher through the gap in the open door. She jumped up to go to his side but was stopped by the quick reaction of the other policeman. In the end it was decided that the interview should be continued at the station as one of the paramedics put his head around the door and said, "It's not looking good for one of them."

Clover House

At the police station Julie was kept in an interview room rather than a cell. Mr Jacobs had been considered as a witness so he was unable to act as 'appropriate adult' for Julie, that task had fallen to Miss Stevenson who arrived at the home just as the police car took Julie away.

They sat together in silence. Miss Stevenson had just been given the basics of what had happened and been asked by the police not to discuss it with Julie. "Can I get you a cup of tea or anything to eat?" asked a female officer that was standing guard at the door. They both declined.

Julie kept asking for an update on Leo's condition, without much response. It was two hours later that a detective entered the room carrying a large file. "I can tell you that Leo French is in hospital and receiving treatment. That is all." He then went on to question Julie for the next hour about what had happened. Between the tears Julie told him the complete story, starting from when she heard the grunting and ending when she picked up the cricket bat. She couldn't remember anything after that.

After going over her statement several times the detective gradually changed his opinion of Julie. Initially he thought of her as someone that had just flipped and started hitting innocent people with a cricket bat. Now she was the heroin of the moment that probably stopped Leo being beaten to death.

Clover House
Chapter 10

Leo Forced open one of his eyes. The swelling made it very difficult. Everything had a tinge of red to it due to the bleeding in his eye. He tried to say something, but like his eyes the swelling around his mouth made speaking almost impossible. He heard a familiar voice telling him not to move and to take things easy. A hand on his shoulder prevented him from attempting to sit upright, along with a sharp pain in his chest when he tried. He dozed back off to sleep.

It was the next day, his third in hospital, before he recovered complete consciousness. His eye, only the one, opened a little easier. Sat next to him was Julie. "Where am I? What happened?" he began to panic due to his unfamiliar surroundings.

"Everything's going to be okay. You just need to rest." Julie wanted to stroke the side of his head or maybe his arm but was scared to do so because everything looked so damaged. "The doctors say you are going to be fine, it will just take time. They say you will need to stay in here another day or so, that's all."

"Where am I?"

"You are in the Leeds General Infirmary. Do you remember what happened?" Julie asked trying

Clover House

to measure if all the bangs to the head had caused any permanent damage.

"Tommy, I remember Tommy being there." The more Leo talked the more he got control of his dry, inflamed lips. "A fight started."

"It's okay Leo, I finished it." Julie tried to change the subject. "Would you like a drink of water?" She poured half a glass full from the jug on the bedside cabinet. As Leo lifted his head to accept it the sharp pain hit him in the chest again.

"Aagh!" He screamed.

"That will be the cracked rib. Tommy did it when he sat on your chest."

"Why did he sit on my chest? What else is wrong with me?" Leo lay back vowing never to move again.

"He was sat on your chest hitting you." Just as Julie was about to list the rest of the injuries, the doctor arrived on his morning visit to the ward. He picked up the clipboard attached to the end of the bed, glanced down at the latest entries and looked over his glasses at Leo.

"And how are we this morning Leo?"

Leo licked his dry lips. "I don't know about you Doc but I feel like shit." This made the doctor smile. A sense of humour was always a good sign.

Clover House

"Has your friend told you what happened?" the doctor asked, giving Julie a sideways glance and looking back down at the clipboard.

"I was in a fight? I think I lost." The doctor smiled again.

"Yes that's right, on both counts. You sustained a deep laceration to your cheek bone, we've stitched that but it will leave you with scar. Fortunately most of the blows you took were to the sides of your face. If he'd have been hitting you straight on, we wouldn't be having this conversation now. You also have a cracked rib that should heal over the next couple of weeks but try and avoid any quick movements. Coughing and sneezing will hurt like hell for a while. Oh yes, your arm will need to be in a sling for a few days, you strained some ligaments in your shoulder. I wouldn't advise looking in the mirror either, not for a day or two. It looks a lot worse than it actually is."

The doctor returned to the end of the bed slid the clipboard back into its holder and pushed his glasses back on to his forehead. "The nurse will bring you some painkillers but all being well you should be able to go home tomorrow. We need the bed this is the NHS you know." At that the doctor swiftly moved on to the next patient.

"What about Tommy?" Leo asked.

Clover House

"What about him?" replied Julie sharply, "Don't you worry about him he got his comeuppance." She knew Leo wouldn't accept that as an answer so she continued. "He's in another hospital, one that specializes in head injuries."

Leo lifted his eyebrows but she didn't elaborate. He wasn't sure he wanted to know anymore, he could guess that Julie had something to do with it. "Why are you looking at me like that? He's had it coming for a long time," said Julie sitting back with her legs and her arms crossed.

Leo was back at Clover House the day before his mother's funeral. The doctor was right the swelling had gone down a little but now all the bruising was coming out. His face was not a pretty sight. Leo spent most of that day in his bedroom talking to Julie. He wasn't in the mood for answering all the other resident's questions and all the stares he would inevitably receive.

"What time is the funeral tomorrow?" Julie asked, although she already knew the answer, she was just trying to make conversation.

"We leave here at 10am. The service starts at 10:30." Leo's reply was in a 'couldn't care less' voice, but Julie could see he was still upset. "Are you coming?" he added.

Clover House

"Of course I'm coming. Why would you ask a question like that?" Julie felt insulted.

"I'm sorry. Like you I'm just making up questions I already know the answer to. You knew the service started at 10:30am."

"Leo I'm going to be there for you every step of the way. I know this isn't going to be easy for you." She moved closer to where he sat on the bed and held him like a child. "And I know what you're thinking?"

"What's that?" he asked.

"That it won't be long before you're attending my funeral." Leo sat up as straight as his bad rib would let him. The thought that went through his head was. This woman has got to go on the fucking stage!

Mr Green helped Leo get washed and dressed. He'd found a smart pair of trousers and a jacket he'd forgotten was even there. The injuries still made it difficult for Leo to do much by himself, though today he had cast off the sling and removed the bandage that covered the cut on his face.

Against doctors' orders he stood in the bathroom looking at himself in the mirror. What a sorry state he was in. He pushed his face closer to look at the deep cut. There must have been at least twenty stitches holding it together. Over his shoulder

Clover House

Mr Green said, "You'll have the women falling over you with a scar like that. You can tell them that you got it fighting off a gang of renegades or that you were the only survivor in a plane crash." Leo wasn't sure if it was something Mr Green had said, all the medication he'd taken to get through the day or something else, for some reason he felt uneasy.

Mr Green fastened Leo's tie and smoothed down a couple of creases in the arms of his jacket. "You look just fine. Your mother would have been proud of you." Leo forced the slightest smile out of the side of his mouth.

"Can you fasten my shoes? I can't bend over because of my rib." He sat back on the bed and held out his leg. Mr Green looked down at the only footwear Leo possessed. It was a pair of Adidas trainers that had seen better days, not at all in keeping with the rest of his clothes. The car would be here in fifteen minutes to pick them up, not enough time to do anything about it. Leo saw the look of disappointment on Mr Green's face. "It's all I have. I know we are supposed to request things like this but they're comfy so I haven't bothered."

"Not a problem. Take mine." Mr Green stood up straight and putting his toe to his heel he shuffled out of his shiny new slip-ons. He bent down and started removing Leo's trainers.

Clover House

"I can't let you do that. You'll look stupid in my trainers," said Leo.

"Nobody will be looking at me. Today is all about you and your mother." He put on the trainers, fastened them and stood up straight. "I see what you mean they are quite comfy," he said smiling, though in truth he was lying, they were at least a size too small.

Julie shouted down the corridor that the car had arrived. Mr Green smiled at Leo and asked if he was ready. "As ready as I'll ever be." They walked out of the bedroom and down the stairs to the hall where Julie and Mr Jacobs were waiting.

Mr Jacobs patted Leo gently on the arm and asked the same question Mr Green had asked. "Are you ready Leo?" Leo replied with the same answer he'd given upstairs. "You look very smart," added Mr Jacobs. He let Julie and Leo lead the way. As Mr Green passed him he whispered. "Pity I couldn't say the same about you. A bit of an effort with the footwear wouldn't have gone amiss."

Outside the chauffer was holding the car door open, the three of them shuffled into the back and Mr Jacobs sat up front with the driver. The car was a stretch limousine, all leather and chrome inside. Leo watched as Julie slid her fingers gently over the fine stitches in the upholstery, then on to the walnut panelling. It was obvious she had never been in such a vehicle before. He was glad she had experienced it, even under these conditions. As it was he that was paying for it, he felt that it was him that had given her the opportunity to taste one of the finer things in life, even if the journey was only fifteen minutes long.

Arriving at the crematorium Julie was surprised to see at least ten cars in the small car park. "It looks like there are a few people here already." Leo's reply was a simple snigger. As the chauffer engaged the hand brake Leo pulled the door handle, got out and began stretching. The chauffer ran around to the other side and opened the doors for the others to exit.

They looked up as a crowd of people came out of the crematorium and headed for the waiting cars. Julie came up alongside Leo and held his hand. They stood and watched them all get into their cars, reverse and drive out in a convoy. Eventually they were the only ones left.

"At least we'll get a seat," joked Leo, as he separated from the others and walked towards the entrance. Julie looked across at Mr Jacobs who replied with a shrug of his shoulders.

"Isn't there anybody else coming?" she asked him in a low voice so Leo couldn't hear.

Clover House

"He, or should I say she, doesn't have any other family and from what I hear she kept herself to herself, no friends." He shrugged his shoulders again as Mr Green walked off in the same direction that Leo had gone, shaking his head from side to side.

"That's so sad," said Julie as she too followed Leo's path.

Inside, the Crematorium had a seating capacity for about one hundred people. The four of them that made up the congregation today sat silently on the front row waiting for something to happen. Eventually the vicar appeared from a back room and walked up to the dais. He welcomed them, though he couldn't help but hide his surprise at how few there were. In his opening speech he got Leo's mother's name slightly wrong, which made Leo giggle, only loud enough for Julie to hear. She squeezed his hand. He wasn't a great believer in God, too many things had happened to him to prevent that.

As the vicar waffled on as though he knew Mrs French like a bosom buddy, Leo's mind drifted back to a conversation he'd once had with a vicar that had visited Clover House. He'd asked him why God gets the credit for all the good things in the World and the devil gets the blame for all the bad things. When Leo was asked to explain he'd said, "Well, look at all the nice things, flowers, birds, scenery, you say God has

Clover House

made all of that, but when a person starts killing people, then that becomes the work of the devil." The vicar was a little flummoxed for a while and gave an explanation that Leo hadn't understood. So Leo had tried to give another example. He asked, "Who causes earthquakes that kill children?"

"You have to appreciate that God works in mysterious ways," replied the vicar.

"What sort of a crock of shit answer is that for all the parents that have lost their children?" demanded Leo. Mr Jacobs had been observing the conversation with interest at a close distance.

"Leo! Apologise now," he'd shouted as he came to the rescue of the vicar. Leo had been mystified as to why it wasn't the vicar who should have been apologising for God. He was supposed to be his voice here on earth.

Leo suddenly snapped back to the present as the others stood up to sing a hymn. Leo didn't recognise the song and he couldn't sing very well anyway. So he did what most people do in church, he mimed. He then noticed for the first time that his mother's coffin was lying on some kind of trolley to one side. How had he not seen that before? He stared at it trying to imagine her inside the plain box. He blinked that thought away as it was too depressing.

Clover House

The rest of the ceremony seemed rushed through. He wondered if the Crematorium was running behind schedule, one reason his mother had waited two weeks for her slot. After a few more prays the coffin was slid on to a conveyer belt, a curtain was opened, leading to who knows where and through it the wooden box went. "Bye mam. Thanks for everything," Leo muttered.

The drive back to Clover House had been in silence. Nobody had even thought about a wake as the low numbers hadn't really justified one. As the car pulled up, Mr Jacobs asked Leo if he was okay, for about the thousandth time. "Yes thanks Mr Jacobs, I'm fine. And thanks for organising everything I really appreciate it." Mr Jacobs nodded in response.

"Fancy swapping shoes back, Mr Green?"

After exchanging footwear Leo had suggested to Julie that they go for a walk. "Those places give me the creeps. I need to blow the cobwebs off." They walked without any purpose or destination for about thirty minutes before Julie asked where they were going, she hadn't been around here before.

"Do you know what I feel like? A drink, that's what," said Leo as he marched off to an off-licence he'd spotted on the corner of the street. Julie felt that this was his day, so if that's what he wanted then he deserved it. They entered the shop to find an ancient looking Asian man behind the counter,

Clover House

reading the local free paper. Julie hung back pretending to look at the crisps down one of the aisles. Leo stood in front of the counter eyeing up the bottles of spirits lined up on the shelf behind the owner. "I'll take a bottle of... whisky, please."

The old man put his paper down and eyed up Leo, "which one? He asked.

It was obvious Leo hadn't done this before because instead of giving a name he pointed to the second shelf and said, "That one with the yellow and red label." Without a word the shopkeeper turned, reached up and took down a bottle of JB whisky.

"That will be £19.99," said the owner in a strong Pakistani accent, holding out his hand. Leo took out a £20 note handed it over and said, "Keep the change."

They had found a small park that was deserted except for the odd person walking their dog. Leo removed his jacket and laid it on the ground. He sat next to it so Julie could use it all. "So now, as I recall it, we have jumped to number five on the wish list, a sip of the devil's brew."

"I forgot about that one," said Julie reading the label on the bottle, "You go first," she said passing Leo the bottle. He unscrewed the lid carefully and put the bottle to his lips. Some of the alcohol got into a slight cut that he still had from the beating, the pain was quite refreshing. He tilted his head back and took a large sip. He immediately regretted taking so much and started coughing and spluttering. Julie went into hysterics.

"I think I may have over indulged on that occasion," Leo said in an over exaggerated, husky voice, "your turn." Julie accepted the bottle, took a deep breath and like Leo tilted her head back.

"Just a minute!" shouted Leo grabbing the bottle out of her hand. "Should you be doing this in your condition?"

Julie grabbed the bottle back. As she put the top to her mouth she asked, "What's it going to do? Kill me?"

"Fair point," said Leo. He had reservations but he kept them to himself. She took a sip but not as big as Leo's.

"Jesus wept," she said with a husky voice she wasn't putting on, "why would anybody drink that for enjoyment?"

"I'm not the expert my mother was, but I think you're supposed to add something to it like lemonade." Leo took the bottle from her and had another swig. This time he was prepared for the taste and swished it around his mouth letting a little go down at a time. It still burnt.

After about an hour they had still only drank a quarter of the bottle between them, but this was

Clover House

sufficient to make them both very merry as they weren't used to drinking alcohol at all. They lay back looking at the clouds that passed overhead. "Can you see a dog in that one?" asked Julie, pointing with a finger that waved from side to side.

"Err no. Can you see a dragon chasing a vicar in that one?" asked Leo, pointing with a similar wavy finger.

"Err no." replied Julie.

After a moment of silence Leo asked, "Where do you think you go when you die?" This question startled Julie. It's something she'd been thinking about a lot since her diagnoses but had never discussed it with anybody. "Do you think my Mam is looking down on us at this very moment?" The word 'moment' was said with a slur brought on by the drink.

Julie realised he was thinking about his mother. She rolled on to her side propped her head up on her hand and asked in a serious and sober voice, "Where do you think we go?"

"I asked first." Leo rolled to face her and mirrored how she was laying.

"You'll laugh if I tell you." She sounded so young and coy. Leo didn't comment, he just waited for her to continue. "I think we go to live on a star." She waited for him to laugh or at least come out with

Clover House

some derisory comment. He still didn't reply. "I was expecting you to laugh or something," she said.

"Why would I laugh? Everybody has their theories. Why should mine be any better or less funny than yours?"

"What is yours? Tell me your theory," she said sounding genuinely interested.

Leo shuffled to make himself comfortable then decided he would be better sat up. "Imagine you are a radio. You are tuned in to one station so you share everything with anybody else tuned into the same frequency." He paused expecting a question. When none was forth coming he carried on. "Like radio frequencies all exist in the same space there are millions of different worlds all existing in the same place at the same time but you are only tuned into one at a time." Again, he paused for a second. When he normally tells people his theory he would have been bombarded with jokes and quips by now. "All scientists agree that we are just made up of energy, and energy can't be destroyed it just changes." He was thinking that he was starting to lose her so he cut it short. "So when we die we stay here, we are just on a different frequency."

After a full minute of thinking Julie put her finger to her lips and said, "I get it." Leo gave a satisfied smile, "so what you are saying is... my dad is now a Radio 2 DJ?"

Clover House

Leo shook his head. "You have gone too far now Julie Sykes." He dived on her and rolled her over in a pretend fight but then gave out a genuine squeal as he rolled onto his cracked rib.

"I'm sorry. Are you okay?" asked Julie.

He rubbed the side of his chest and the pain soon went. "Pass me that bottle. I need some pain killer."

Leo was drinking more than Julie. Often when she put the bottle to her mouth she was only pretending to drink. She was still quite tipsy so agreed with Leo when he suggested that they can now tick off number five on the wish list. She had enjoyed her afternoon in the park but believes she would have enjoyed it just as much with Leo and without the whisky. Even though Leo's theory about what happens to you when you die sounded more plausible than hers, she was sticking with her belief that this time next year she would inhabit her own little star.

Walking back to Clover House the conversation returned to Julie's wish list. "So which have we done, and what's still to do?" Leo asked. Julie once again retrieved the list from her back pocket and unfolded the scrap of paper.

"We have done numbers, one, two and five, which means we still have number three," she hesitated before saying what it was as it all sounded a bit stupid now. "Touching the palm tree shadow on the sand, number four the skinny dipping, but I'm not sure about that one now, and number six."

"You never did tell me what number six was," said Leo.

"And I'm not going to either," replied Julie folding the sheet back up and putting it away.

"Why the hesitation over the skinny dipping? That's probably one of the easiest to organise," said Leo with a mischievous grin.

Changing the subject Julie asked, "Shall we just forget the palm tree thing, it sounds stupid, as well as impossible."

"How dare you doubt my ability to perform the impossible? I've been thinking about that one and I have an idea. Do you have a passport?"

Julie thought for a second. "I'm not sure."

"When we get back I may need your help to distract Mr Jacobs, that's if he's there of course." Leo picked up the pace and Julie had to do a little trot every so often to keep up.

Clover House
Chapter 11

Entering the house Leo looked around the door from the hall to see if Mr Jacobs was in his office. He was sat reading a newspaper with a set of headphones on. Leo knew he enjoyed reading the paper whilst listening to classical music. "We need an excuse to get him out of his office for a while."

"Why, what are you planning to do?" asked Julie. Leo replied with a tap to the side of his nose.

"I need him out of his office for about ten minutes." He thought the less Julie knows the better. Without saying another word Julie left Leo's side and walked up to Mr Jacobs's office door. She banged her knuckles against the door jam. No response. Julie took a step inside and started waving her arms to get his attention. Eventually he looked up and removed the headphones.

"Yes, what can I do for you Julie?" he said closing the newspaper.

"I have something amazing to show you Mr Jacobs. Please come and see." She waited for him to make a move before leading the way. She led him through the hallway, past Leo and straight outside. For extra time Leo flicked the lock on the inside of the front door. He was curious what she was going to show him that was so interesting.

Clover House

Knowing his time was limited Leo made straight for the office and closed the door behind him quietly. The last thing he wanted was someone like Charlie catching him. He moved swiftly over to the desk and pulled open the single drawer to the left. It held only stationery. He opened the drawer on the right. This was filled with knickknacks, including everything from a half-eaten packet of Polo mints to a pair of cufflinks. Then he spotted what he was looking for: a single key. He grabbed it and turned to face the filing cabinet. He slid the key into the hole at the top and turned it slowly. Once it had turned a full circle he tried one of the drawers, it opened silently on its runners. The drawer was full of even more stationery, photocopy paper, boxes of Bic pens, Crystal files. This isn't what he was expecting. He closed that drawer and looked down at the labels on the others. The second drawer down had a label that read-

'RESIDENTS'.

Pulling this one open he found exactly what he was looking for. Each file had a tab on top with the name of a different resident. He used his fingers to flick through each one, there it was, 'FRENCH. L.' He pulled out the file. Most of the contents were just letters and reports. He would have loved to have read them all but there just wasn't time. Then he saw what he'd been looking for, a bank statement.

Clover House

He removed this and was just about to put the file back when he thought of something else. He went through the contents for a second time and just when he was about to give up hope he saw it sticking out of an envelope, a passport. Never in a million years did he really expect to find one, why would he own a passport?

Time was running out for Leo so he quickly let his fingers flick through the tabs once again, SYKES. J. This is it. He pulled out the file and was surprised to find that it was nearly twice as thick as his, even though Julie had only been at the home for less than a couple of months. He assumed that most of it referred to her medical condition. Luck was on his side, right at the front was a similar envelope to his containing a passport. Like his, he left it in the file for a later date. He returned her file to the cabinet, making sure he put it in the right place, the whole drawer had been organised alphabetically. He returned the key to the desk drawer, again putting it back exactly where he'd found it. Leo went to the office door and opened it ever so slightly to make sure nobody was about. The coast was clear, so he stepped out.

"Do you know Julie, all the time I've been here and I've never noticed that before. Thank you for bringing it to my attention, most interesting," said Mr Jacobs as he re-entered the house. He was

Clover House

holding a bunch of keys, presumably the ones he'd used to get back in.

"I knew you'd be impressed," said Julie whilst looking directly at Leo. Mr Jacobs nodded at Leo as he passed him and went straight back into his office.

She waited for him to get out of ear shot before asking Leo what all that was about. "Just you wait and see," he replied. "The miracle worker has started to weave his magic. By the way what was it you showed him that was so interesting?"

"Your four leaf clovers," she said, almost apologetically.

"That was our secret, but I forgive you. I think it will be worth it," he said with a smile and a wink.

Clover House seemed a lot more relaxed now Tommy Bishop wasn't lording it over everybody and everything. Meal times were much more enjoyable with people feeling free to express a comment without fear of repercussions. Nobody mentioned him or what had happened to him, they were all just thankful for the respite as no one knew how long it would last.

Poor little Johnny Fish was particularly grateful. He had drawn the short straw and had been sharing a bedroom with Tommy for quite some time now. All Tommy's things were still in the room so Johnny wasn't counting his chickens just yet. Like

Clover House

everyone else he was making the most of it. One other thing had changed since Tommy's departure, nobody messed with Julie Sykes.

It had taken Leo a few days to work out where the nearest branch was of the bank where his money had been deposited. As it turned out it was just one hundred yards from the arcade he visited nearly every week. He'd put on his best jacket and trousers again and sneaked out the back door of the home, this is something he wanted to do alone.

Once inside the bank he joined the short queue to the cashier. He glanced around looking at the security cameras, all the while feeling guilty. He didn't know why he should feel this way, he wasn't robbing the bank, just withdrawing some of his own money. When it was his turn a pleasant looking girl smiled from the other side of the glass partition and asked what she could do for him. "I'd like to draw one thousand pounds out of my account please."

"Right, has this been pre-requested?" she asked, still wearing the smile.

"I'm sorry. I have no idea what you mean." Leo was beginning to think this may have been a bad idea.

"Have you already spoken to somebody and told them you are coming to collect it?" She was now speaking slower as though he was either slightly deaf or a bit thick.

Clover House

"No. I have this with all my details on." He slid the bank statement under the small gap between them. She picked it up and glanced at the details.

"And you are Leo French?" she asked. Leo thought this a stupid question.

"Do you have any photo ID with you?" Leo was now regretting not taking the passports when he had the chance. He fished around in his pockets. The people in the queue behind him were becoming restless.

"I have this." He produced a bus pass that most of the residents at the home had been issued with.

"We normally require either a passport or a driver's licence." The girl's smile had vanished. Leo thought for a moment, looked over his shoulder at the queue that was now getting longer, then back at the girl.

"But I don't have either so what am I to do when I want my money," he lied.

"Don't you have a banker's card?" Not only had the girl's smile gone but she was becoming irritated.

"No."

"Please wait here." The girl scooped up his statement and bus pass and disappeared behind another partition. The sigh from the rest of the queue was audible.

Ten minutes later she returned with her supervisor. She sat in her seat and the supervisor

Clover House

leant over her shoulder towards the glass partition. "Mr French can I ask why you need the money?" It was Leo's turn to be irritated.

"No you can't ask what it's for. It's personal." The queue found this quite amusing. "I just want some of my money that you are holding for me, why should I have to jump through all these hoops?" The queue behind him applauded. Looking deflated the supervisor threw down the statement and bus pass onto the cashier's desk and said, "Just give him the money." She then disappeared back behind her internal partition. Once again the queue burst into applause. Leo turned and took a bow.

Walking down the road with one thousand pounds in his pocket. Leo felt like the king of the world. He felt like he'd just won the lottery. He knew that one day he would have to answer to Mr Jacobs for his actions, but right this minute he couldn't give a damn.

He sneaked back in using the rear door and up the stairs to his bedroom. Once inside he closed the door and knelt down at the side of his bed. He was just about to lift the faulty floorboard where he hid his money when he heard his bedroom door open behind him. He quickly put his elbows on the bed placed his hands together and started saying, "Dear

Clover House

Lord please look after my Mam I know she can be a bit of a pain..."

"I'm sorry Leo I should have knocked," said Julie leaving and shutting the door behind her.

"Come back here you silly mare. You gave me the fright of my life. I thought you were a member of staff." Julie re-entered the room a little confused. Leo lifted the faulty floorboard and removed an old coffee jar.

"What are you doing?" Julie asked kneeling besides him. Leo emptied the contents of the jar onto the floor. About forty pounds in notes and another five in coins danced on the floor. Without saying a word he took the one thousand pounds out of his jacket pocket and forced it into the jar. Julie moved away as though the money was infected.

"Where the hell did you get all that from?"

"I robbed a bank." Leo had to correct himself quickly, he could see that Julie actually believed him, "It's mine. I overheard Mr Jacobs and that cow, Mrs Westland talking about my mother's funeral in the office. They said that I had over seven thousand pounds in the bank and that would pay for it." Julie relaxed a little. Leo continued, "That's why I needed you to distract Mr Jacobs the other day, so I could get the details and draw some out.

"Why would you need so much? All you will do is spend it all at the arcade." Julie was confused

Clover House

again. Leo smiled he couldn't wait to see the expression on her face when he told her what he was going to do with it.

"Not this time Julie. This...," he held up the jar, "...is number three." He waited for the penny to drop. When it did her face was a picture. "Oh and by the way, you do have a passport."

Charlie had been walking behind Julie when she'd inadvertently walked in and found Leo hiding his money. Hearing the two of them talking Charlie peeped through the gap in the door. He couldn't believe his eyes when he saw the money spread around the coffee jar on Leo's bedroom floor. When Leo brought the rest out of his pocket his eyes had nearly popped out of his head, he'd never seen so much money in one place before.

He returned to his own bedroom and closed the door leaving it open just enough so that he could see Leo's. He waited fifteen minutes before he eventually saw Julie and Leo leave and go downstairs. He waited another five minutes in case they had forgotten something and returned, he didn't want to get caught.

He tip-toed across the hall, opened Leo's door, entered and quietly closed it behind him. Charlie hadn't been at Clover House long or he would have known that one of the deadly sins is to enter someone else's room without permission. The

Clover House

residents didn't have much privacy but what they did have they valued above all else. To be honest if Charlie had known the unwritten rule then he would probably have still done it, the reward was so great.

Once inside he placed his back against the door and scanned the bedroom for a clue as to where the coffee jar may be hidden. He searched the drawers of the dresser, the wardrobe, in fact every nook and cranny he could reach, all the time being careful not to disturb anything too much.

He was just about to give up when he took a step backwards to see if he could see anything on top of the wardrobe. As he did he felt the floorboard creak beneath his left foot, he pivoted back and forward to reproduce the noise. He was smiling before he'd even looked down.

Lifting the loose fitting section of floor board, Charlie put his hand inside and moved it this way and that. Accidently he knocked over the jar. He had to go elbow deep before he could get a firm hold of the container. Bringing it out of its hiding place the coins all slid and jangled together. Charlie froze and looked at the door anybody passing at that moment would have heard the noise. He wouldn't have known what to do if Leo had walked back in, catching him red handed.

Knowing he was on borrowed time Charlie reached into the jar and pulled out the roll of bank

Clover House

notes, held together by a single elastic band. He left the change he just couldn't risk the noise it might make if he tipped it out.

Charlie pushed the notes into his jeans pocket, screwed the lid back on and replaced the jar. Finally he put the piece of floorboard back into position, stood up and looked around making sure everything was just as he had found it. He was working on the principle that if Leo thought the money was safe then it could be days or even weeks before he noticed it had gone.

Charlie opened the door just a crack to make sure the coast was clear. After looking both ways he stepped in to the corridor and closed the door, just as Fish came around the corner.

"Hi Charlie, what are you up to?" asked Fish.

"Nothing, I'm not doing anything," replied Charlie.

"Okay, okay, keep your hair on. It's just a turn of phrase." Fish continued down the corridor to his own room.

Julie and Leo were watching a TV show where it seemed couples came on to fight out their differences. A large man with ungainly hair, tattoos, a massive beer belly and very few teeth was in the middle of two women fighting over him.

"Do you think we'll ever argue like that?" asked Leo.

Clover House

"Don't tell me you are seeing Mary on the side," asked Julie pretending to be upset.

"Okay, I won't tell you I'll just keep on doing it," said Leo.

"In your dreams," muttered Mary, sat to one side reading another celebrity magazine, she didn't even look up.

A security guard had to come on to the stage to separate the two women who were now pulling each other's hair. You couldn't hear any dialogue as the producers had beeped out the shouted conversation due to the bad language. The host of the show loved it.

As the program finished, and without asking anybody else's opinion, Leo picked up the remote control and switched the channel over. "Hey I was watching that," said Julie.

"What? There was nothing on but adverts." Leo selected the history channel to watch a program he'd been waiting for about the RAF. Right on cue the Red Arrows did their popular split manoeuvre, leaving a trail of smoke in red, white and blue. Julie was sure she could hear him humming like a jet engine under his breath.

Following the Red Arrows in a display formation were several World War Two bombers. "Look, those are like the ones on my 50p piece." For a second Leo couldn't remember where he had left

Clover House

the precious coin. He started tapping the outside of his pockets with the palms of his hands.

"What have you lost?" asked Julie.

"My lucky 50p piece. I can't remember where I put it." Leo continued searching.

"You and your memory. You tipped all your change into the coffee jar with all your other ill-gotten gains," said Julie shaking her head side to side.

"That's right. I'd better get it before I spend it by mistake. Thanks, what would I do without you?" He bent over and kissed Julie's forehead before leaving.

Inside the bedroom he closed the door and removed the floorboard. Reaching underneath his heart stopped for a minute when he couldn't feel the jar in its usual place, about a foot in and to the left. He swung his arm left and then right where he eventually found it. Bringing it out of the dark hole he stared in disbelief, the money from the bank had gone. In fact all the notes had gone just the change sat at the bottom of the jar.

He unscrewed the top and poured the money into his hand, his lucky 50p was there but that seemed little consolation now.

Leo put the 50p into his pocket and started making his way down the stairs. At the bottom in the

Clover House

hall he bumped into Fish. "You've not seen anyone near my bedroom have you?" he asked.

"Funny you should say that, I saw Charlie skulking in the corridor looking very suspicious not long ago. Why what's he been up to?"

"Nothing I hope. Thanks Fish." Leo walked off.

Leo joined Julie in the lounge. His TV program had been replaced with a soap opera in his absence. "Did you want me to turn it back over?" she asked pointing the remote at the TV.

Ignoring the question Leo moved closer, out of earshot of Mary. "It's gone."

"What's gone? Your lucky 50p piece? That's a shame you told me you were going to keep that forever."

"Not the 50p, the thousand pounds I withdrew from the bank." Leo whispered.

"Eh. What?" Leo signalled for her to keep her voice down by nodding towards Mary. Julie continued to panic. "But we only put it there half an hour ago, where could it possibly have gone?"

"Fish said he saw Charlie looking suspicious in the corridor outside my bedroom earlier," Leo looked on the verge of tears.

"That little..." said Julie at a loss to find a suitable word to finish her sentence. "What are you going to do?" she could hear the cogs turning in Leo's mind.

Clover House

"We have to know it's him first. We can't report the theft because we weren't supposed to have the money in the first place." Leo was hatching a plan.

Charlie walked into the lounge. Looking up he saw Leo and thought about doing a U-turn. "Hi Charlie, come and join us," shouted Leo. Charlie looked around the room for an escape route but decided to bluff it out, Leo couldn't possibly know about the missing money already. Could he?

Leo and Julie parted letting Charlie sit on the sofa between them. "How's it going Charlie, are you settling in?" asked Julie.

Charlie knew there was something wrong but he carried on as normal as possible. "Everything's fine. My mother is out of hospital in two days so I'll be going home."

"Are you sure about that?" asked Leo.

"Mr Jacobs told me this morning so I'm guessing its right," said Charlie hesitantly.

"Didn't Mr Jacobs tell you about the Assessment Test though?" asked Leo.

"What test?" asked Charlie, he had no idea what they were talking about. This was all news to him.

Leo explained, "I thought everyone knew about 'The Test'. Everybody who comes to Clover House, or any other Social Services Centre come to that, is

Clover House

continually monitored to see if they should be allowed home and back in to society." Charlie spun his head to look at Julie and when he did Leo winked at her behind his back.

"Maybe they didn't tell you about it Charlie because you're so much younger than most of us here. You're a tricky character and just maybe you could cheat the test and pass it when you should have failed," said Julie taking Leo's lead.

Charlie started biting his nails then asked, "What does this test entail then?"

Julie smiled at him, "Well Leo has been here the longest so obviously he's on the judging panel. It's like he said, it's just to make sure that you're a reliable and trustworthy person that can be let back into Society."

"But my mother's coming for me" stated Charlie. Julie was convinced she saw his bottom lip start to quiver.

Leo continued, in fact he was starting to enjoy this a little. "I'm afraid it goes beyond your mother's decision, a higher authority you might say." Charlie didn't understand but he didn't want to admit it.

It was Leo's turn to smile at Charlie, giving him the impression he was on his side. "You will be judged on things like your work ethic, how much you help others whilst here. How you've looked after yourself. Have you cleaned your teeth today Charlie?"

Charlie made a large swallowing noise, "Err no," he admitted.

"And of course how honest you are." Leo had never been fishing but imagined that this must be what it's like as you reel in a nice big one. "That's an important one, if not the most important, honesty."

"What do you mean?" Charlie eyes were now starting to fill and Julie was wondering if they were going too far.

"Well we can't let people out into Society if they aren't honest. I think you'd agree with that Charlie. That just wouldn't be right. You are an honest person aren't you Charlie?" There was another big swallowing sound.

Charlie could feel his mouth going dry. "You're both just messing with me, you're kidding?"

"We'll see when I have the meeting with the other judges before your mother comes to take you home. I'm sorry Charlie but if anything comes out in that meeting that let's say, proves you're a dishonest person, then you will spend the rest of your life here at Clover House." To scare him a little more Leo added, "That's why I have to stay here for the rest of my life. They found out that I'd stolen a pound coin from the charity box on the telephone table in the hall."

Clover House

Charlie could feel the roll of bank notes in his pocket almost burning through his flesh. If Leo had to stay here for stealing just one pound coin, what would happen to him?

Charlie stood up from the sofa and looked at Leo and Julie, giving them one last chance to feed him the punch line and tell him this was one big joke. "Better go and clean your teeth," said Julie in a dismissive manner, then she changed all her attention on to the television.

"Okay I'll go and do them now," said Charlie. As he left the room both Leo and Julie fell about in fits of laughter.

Mary put down her magazine and said, "There isn't really a test, is there?"

Charlie crept back up the stairs and into Leo's bedroom, he didn't hang around to see if anybody was watching he just wanted to get the money back where it belonged, before the judges found out he'd taken it.

As he screwed the lid back on and replaced the floorboard he consoled himself with the fact that the money probably wouldn't be any good to him anyway. Especially when you consider that he's not allowed to even go to the shops on his own.

Later that day after checking the money had been returned Leo decided that a little homework

Clover House

would be in order. He wasn't going to repeat the mistakes from the Manchester trip. This time he was going to research this excursion properly. He positioned himself at the computer terminal, hands poised over the keyboard, safe in the knowledge that Tommy wasn't going to surprise him from behind. He brought up the 'maps' page and centred the UK in the middle, it looked tiny. His eyes drifted down to Spain then he pushed the button to zoom in closer. The name Malaga then caught his attention, he'd often heard that place mentioned when people spoke about holidays they'd been on. He zoomed in even closer. "Well at least it has an airport," he said to himself. He came out of the 'maps' and went into Google. He typed the letters M-A-L-A-G-A, and hit the enter key, up popped a whole list of sites offering places to stay and suggesting things to do. He knew what he wanted to do and he didn't intend staying. If possible this excursion had to be a day trip, there and back before anybody noticed they were missing.

Now, how to get there? Flying was the obvious choice, it may not be the cheapest but in this case speed was of the essence. He returned to the Google search page and typed in 'Flights to Malaga' an array of travel companies came up, but the one most mentioned was Ryan Air. He clicked on their Home Page, up came a list of options. He spent the next thirty minutes ticking boxes, choosing dates, destination, luggage, insurance etc. When it was all filled in it produced a price of one hundred and sixty pounds each for a return flight. The site asked, 'Would you like to book this?' He clicked yes. The next page was the 'booking details'. It was when his eyes caught the question at the bottom of the page that his heart sank. The question was 'Which card would you like to use, Debit or Credit?'

At breakfast the next day he waited until everyone had been served and was chomping into their bacon and egg sandwiches. Leo turned to Julie and explained what he had found out on the computer and the fact that he had hit a snag because he didn't have a Credit or Debit card. "I don't suppose you have one?" he asked.

"Sorry, no," she replied. "But there is another option. We can book the flights at a Travel Agent's." This was so obvious to Leo he couldn't understand why he hadn't thought of it.

"Okay tomorrow that's what we'll do. If anybody asks we are going to the arcade." Julie wasn't sure why he'd added that because nobody ever did ask where you were going.

After breakfast the next day, armed with a printout from the Ryan Air site Leo and Julie marched into the travel agents on the high street. They had to

Clover House

wait a few minutes to be served but when the lady invited them to take a seat they were like a couple of excited school children. "What can I do for you?" she asked. Leo pulled the printout from his jacket pocket and laid it on the desk in front of her.

"I would like to book these flights please," Leo said pushing the sheet towards her.

The lady, Barbara according to her name badge, read the sheet, glanced at her colleagues on either side and leant forward. In not more than a whisper she said, "You would get them cheaper booking them on line. Doing it through us will cost you a little more than the prices shown here."

"I realise that," said Leo. "But I don't possess any Credit or Debit cards. That's why we've come here." Barbara nodded, reread the sheet and starting typing things into the computer. Eventually she swivelled the monitor round so they both could read it and started going through what she'd entered. The price was a little more, but that didn't matter, he could afford it.

Walking back to Clover House Leo danced around Julie waving the confirmation like a game show host tempting a contestant, "yes madam here in my hot little hand I have two, yes two tickets to sunny Spain." She made a grab for them but he was too quick. She suddenly stopped and turned all serious. "Everything is going to be okay, isn't it?"

Clover House

Leo stopped just ahead of her, lowered the tickets and adopted a serious manner also. "Of course everything is going to be fine. I've double checked all the times, transfers, cost in fact everything. The only thing that can go wrong with this trip is a hurricane or a nuclear war.

"You said that about Manchester, and we got into quite a dodgy situation there if you remember," Julie frowned.

"It worked out well in the end though." Leo was smiling but then realised Julie wasn't. "Seriously, we have more money to do it this time, and I've learnt my lesson." Julie did that thing where she smiles out of one side of her mouth, the most none committal smile Leo had ever seen.

"So what time do we set off?" she asked.

"Tuesday morning we rise at 06:15 precisely." Both Leo's eyes looked up and to the right, as if that's where he kept his memory. "We catch a taxi on the High Street at approximately 06:47."

"06:47? That is precise," Julie said interrupting him.

"Like I said Miss Sykes, nothing is being left to chance."

Tuesday morning came and Julie was up early, dressed and ready for 05:30. It took several knocks on Leo's bedroom door to muster him, especially

Clover House

when she had to do it without waking the rest of the house. He opened the door and put his head round looking quite dreary.

"Aren't you ready yet? I've been up for ages," demanded Julie.

"Why what's happening, what time is it? Leo rubbed his eyes. Julie was just about to give him a piece of her mind and storm off when he opened the door wide and said "Tah da!" There he was stood completely dressed with a rucksack in his hand. "All ready," he declared.

"That's not funny. My stomach is churning so I can do without your pranks today."

"Sorry," he relented. "Have you got everything ready, suntan lotion, sunglasses?" She hadn't even thought of anything like that but wasn't going to admit to him that she wasn't prepared.

"Don't worry I've got everything I need, as long as you have," she said.

"I just need to grab the passports on the way out," said Leo closing his bedroom door slowly waiting for the click.

"You haven't got the passports out of Mr Jacobs's office yet?" She wasn't sure if he was just winding her up again or not.

"I couldn't get them too early, he might have found them missing and that would have blown the

Clover House

whole trip." She hated to do it but she admitted that he was right.

Julie waited by the front door while Leo sneaked into the Manager's office. For a moment he wondered what he would have done if the office door had been locked, he brushed that thought away with a shudder. Once inside he knew exactly where to go for the filing cabinet key and where to look inside the drawer. First he found Julie's passport then he recovered his own. Lastly he replaced the key in the desk drawer and closed it quietly.

"What are you doing?" Leo nearly had a heart attack. Julie repeated herself "What are you doing? Come on we have a plane to catch." Leo put his hand to his chest to make sure his heart was still beating, took a deep breath then followed Julie out.

Like before Leo closed the large front door behind him waiting for the click, the last thing they needed was someone catching them and asking questions now. At the gate Julie paused, bent down and picked a four leaf clover from the lawn. She smiled at Leo, tucked the leaf into her blouse pocket and said, "I think we will need all the luck we can get today."

Leo shook his head from side to side. "Oh ye of little faith," he replied. What Julie couldn't see was Leo's fingers crossed behind his back.

Clover House

At the taxi rank on the High Street there was just one car waiting. The driver was sat inside reading a newspaper. Leo tapped on his window to get his attention then opened the back door for Julie to get in. "Leeds Bradford Airport, please mate," said Leo as though he did this every morning. He slid in next to her and closed the door.

"Going somewhere nice?" asked the driver.

"Malaga," said Leo, immediately regretting telling the driver their destination. In Leo's experience you only told people what they needed to know. For the rest of the journey they had to listen to the driver explaining the virtues of holidaying in the UK. "None of that rubbish food and foreign lingo. Then you have to change your money." Unfortunately Leo had switched off by now, something he was to regret before the day was over.

Arriving at the airport they got out of the taxi and Leo paid the driver. He even included a small tip. As the car drove off they both turned and faced the terminal building, which looked quite intimidating. People were dashing in and out of the rotating doors, adults were shouting at children to keep up as they dragged large suitcases behind them. Businessmen in suits were forever checking their watches. Even Leo started to feel nervous now. A pilot proudly wearing the gold bands on the sleeve of his jacket passed

Clover House

them pulling a small overnight case, behind him four beautiful Flight attendants, all wearing the same the uniform followed him like a pack of groupies.

"Where do we go now?" asked Julie, fascinated by the hustle and bustle of the terminals corridors.

Leo scanned the immediate area then saw what he was looking for. A small group of people were huddled under a bank of TV monitors. He grabbed Julie's hand so as not to lose her. "Over here," he said dragging her towards them. Leo took his booking confirmation from his pocket and compared it to the numbers shown on the screens. "There," he said pointing to the screen that said departures. "Flight FR2446 to Malaga. Check in 14 Gate 6."

"What does all that mean?" asked Julie waiting for a full explanation.

"I have no idea," confessed Leo shaking his head and looking down at his booking sheet. "There's a Ryan Air desk over there, we'll ask them." They joined the short queue awaiting their turn.

"It's not my fault the plane went without me. There was a hold up on the motorway," shouted an angry passenger at the front of the queue.

"Good job we got here two hours before the flight," Leo whispered to Julie.

Clover House

The dispute between the passenger and the airline staff went on for another fifteen minutes without any progress. Eventually the passenger stormed off vowing never to use their airline again. The next person's question was answered quickly and easily so now it was the turn of Leo and Julie.

"Can I help you?" asked the pleasant looking man behind the counter. Leo smiled back.

"Yes. We are new to flying and wondered what we should do now we have arrived at the airport." The man hesitated, wondering if they were joking. When Leo said nothing else the man replied.

"Can I see your flight confirmation sir?" Leo pulled the sheet from his jacket pocket and handed it over. "Are yes, you need to check in at desk fourteen. Have you checked in on-line sir?"

"Err, what do you mean?" The man's smile disappeared as he glanced down at the booking form again.

"Unfortunately if you haven't checked in on-line for this flight it is going to cost you an additional £70...each."

"What the fuck!" said Leo, then realised he was starting to sound like the passenger he'd been listening to earlier.

"I'm sorry sir. The confirmation clearly states that you have to book in on-line and can print your boarding pass up to two hours before the flight. How

Clover House

would you like to pay the £140?" Leo knew he didn't have a choice so he counted out the money and handed it over. He looked at Julie with an expression that said, I know, don't say anything.

"What about the return flight?" Leo thought he'd drawn plenty of money out when he asked for one thousand pounds at the bank, now he was thinking he should have asked for more.

"There is a booth over there that lets you check in and print your boarding pass. I would do it now if I were you, for your return flight." The man pointed a finger over Leo's shoulder. Leo waited for the printer to produce their boarding passes, accepted them and walked straight over to the booth the man had pointed out. Julie waited outside.

Ten minutes later Leo emerged. "I'm glad everything's going to run like clockwork," Julie said wearing a mischievous grin. Leo ignored her and started walking over to the desk that had yet another queue, above the desk it read RYANAIR-MALAGA.

When it was their turn a young woman said, "Hello. Can I see your tickets and passports please?" Leo handed over the two passports, the booking form and the boarding passes he'd just paid £140 for. "You don't have any cases booked on sir." Leo wasn't sure if this was a question or a statement.

"No we are just taking our rucksacks." He held his up to show her.

Clover House

"That's fine sir. It's just that you only have to check in here if you have luggage. Otherwise you can go straight through to Security down the corridor." He didn't even turn to look at Julie. He knew exactly what her expression would be. He led the way towards Security following the signs. Along the way they were stopped by a young man who asked to see their boarding passes. He swiped them under a scanner then waved them on. As they turned the corner they entered a large room with yet another queue, though this one seemed to be moving a little faster.

Julie sidled up alongside Leo. "Why is everyone taking their belts and shoes off? Leo became all authoritative. This at last was something he had read up on.

"It's just a simple search procedure. Making sure you aren't taking anything on board the plane that you're not allowed to take. You have to place the contents from your pockets into the plastic containers, as well as belts, shoes, jewellery and of course your jacket and rucksack."

"Then what happens to it?" Julie was fascinated.

"It goes through the X-ray machine and you collect it on the other side."

"What are those people doing?" Julie was watching people go through the large scanner that

Clover House

detects anything you may still have on your person. Leo explained this to her then told her there was nothing to worry about.

As they got closer the line divided into three separate ones where Julie and Leo became separated. He mouthed the words to her 'see you on the other side' and gave her a wave. Like everyone else he removed his shoes along with his jacket and belt and placed them all in the container. Julie's line was moving a little faster and he watched as she copied the person in front of her, placing her belongings on the short conveyer belt.

Looking across he saw Julie walking through the large scanner, it beeped he frowned. She was asked to walk through it once more, it beeped again. The female security guard started speaking to her and sliding a black stick up and down her body. When the security guard realised Julie was still wearing her watch and St Christopher she asked her to remove them and once again walk through the scanner. A green light came on above it, she continued walking. Leo sighed.

It was now Leo's turn. His queue was at the walk-through scanner. He waved to Julie who was waiting for him on the other side looking for her plastic container. As Leo passed through the scanner beeped. He patted his pockets convinced he hadn't left anything inside, he then checked for his watch. A

Clover House

burly security guard walked up to him. "Do you have anything in your pockets, Sir?" Like the one that searched Julie, he too was sliding a black wand up and down Leo's body. It beeped as it travelled over his hip. Leo then remembered what it was. He kept his lucky 50p piece that Julie had given him in the tiny hip pocket on his jeans. He didn't want to spend it by accident. He removed it and put it on the shelf next to him, the guard continued scanning him.

Hearing a commotion Leo looked up to see Julie being escorted away by two security guards, one carrying the plastic container that held all her belongings.

"Leo, help me," she screamed.

The guard examining Leo also looked across from where the scream was coming from, he then looked back at Leo. "Are you travelling with that young lady, sir?" As he asked the question the hand held metal detector let out a beep. Not waiting for an answer to his question the guard ran the wand over Leo's thigh again, there was another beep only this time it was continuous. The guard calmly stood up straight, nodded to a couple of colleagues and grabbed Leo's arm.

It all seemed to happen so quickly. Leo was now sat in an empty room, that was except for the table and four chairs all screwed to the floor. In walked the security guard that searched him along

Clover House

with another man wearing a shirt and tie. "Well Mr French it would appear that we need to see what is beneath your trousers and thought it would be better doing it somewhere a little more private."

"Beneath my trousers? What are you talking about I don't have anything beneath my trousers. I want to know what is happening to my friend that you dragged off."

"Come, come Mr French we didn't drag anyone 'off'." This man reminded Leo of a Bond villain. He was expecting him to produce a long haired white cat and start stroking it.

"She certainly didn't want to go with your lot." Leo began to stand.

"I'm sure this matter can be resolved. Would you mind removing your trousers sir?" Leo looked at the other guard and knew he wasn't going to get out of here without doing what the man asked, and the sooner he did it the sooner they could be on their way, he had nothing to hide.

Without realising it Julie was in the room adjacent to Leo's, only she had two females questioning her. "Do you know the rules Miss Sykes what is and what isn't allowed on an aircraft?" The one doing the questioning had a pad in front of her as well as Julie's processions.

"Not really I haven't flown before." Julie looked scared stiff. "Where's my friend?"

Clover House

"Mr French is being questioned." Julie started to panic. "Do you know that sharp objects are not allowed on flights of any kind?" Julie thought for a minute. She had no idea to what they were referring.

"Look if I have something I shouldn't have I'm sorry, like I said I haven't flown before all this is new to me. Can't you just take it off me and let me carry on." The two females questioning Julie looked at each other. Then one said. "Normally Miss Sykes we would, but first we need an explanation as to what it is our X-ray machine picked up." Julie was puzzled.

Leo removed his trousers and placed them on the back of the chair. The guard brought over his hand scanner and began running it up and down the trousers as he held them up. The machine remained silent.

The man in the shirt and tie instructed the guard to go over Leo's leg with the scanner. Leo obliged by putting his foot on the seat of the chair. The guard was just about to turn the scanner back on when he hesitated and called his colleague over. The two men looked down at the scar. "How did you do this Mr French?"

"I don't remember it was years ago." Leo placed his hand over it, he was embarrassed.

"You don't remember getting an injury like that?" asked the tie wearer. "Do you know if they

Clover House

put any metal pins inside when you sustained the injury?"

"I told you I don't remember." After receiving a nod the guard turned on the hand held metal detector and ran it over the scar. It beeped continuously again.

As if by magic the female guard questioning Julie produced a syringe with a covered needle attached. "This is not only classed as a sharp object, we also need to know its contents. I'm sure you are aware Miss Sykes we take drugs very seriously."

Now she knew what they had been talking about Julie's shoulders slumped with relief. "That. That's my medication."

"Medication for what? To carry needles on board an aircraft you have to have a doctor's certificate and they have to be locked away by the Flight attendants during flight.

"I'm sorry I didn't know that. It's part of my cancer treatment." The posture of the two women changed at hearing that one word.

"Is there someone we can check this with?" Even the guard's voice sounded more sympathetic. Julie didn't want to give them the details of the Doctor treating her or the number for Clover House. As soon as they received a call from Security at the airport they will put a stop to the journey.

Clover House

"I'm sorry I don't carry my Doctor's telephone number, but if you look in the side pocket of my rucksack there are some tablets along with an appointment card for my next visit." Without saying a word the female guard picked the rucksack out of the plastic tray. She spun it around until the front pocket faced her. After unzipping it carefully she peered in to the small pocket. Once she knew there were no more needles or anything else in the pocket that could cause damage she put her hand in and withdrew a small plastic bottle containing tablets, she read the label. She placed the bottle on the table and put her hand back into the pocket, this time she brought out an appointment card. The card was headed ONCOLOGY Department Leeds General Infirmary. The appointment was in four days' time. The guard had been to this department with her sister only last month so she knew Julie was telling the truth. "Okay Julie let me go and have a word with my supervisor." The guard that had been doing all the talking left the room, leaving the other to watch Julie and her possessions.

When she returned she said, "Julie, we have a slight problem. My Supervisor said we can let you continue the journey but unfortunately not with the syringe. So if it is medication you are going to need then obviously you won't be able to go." The demeanour of the guard had changed, she even sounded apologetic. Julie responded quickly with a white lie.

"No I don't need it today, I've had a shot this morning so I'm not due one until tomorrow. I only brought that as a spare." Julie knew she would be back by evening and that is when it was really due. The guard looked at her, not totally convinced.

"Only if you're sure. We wouldn't want you falling ill. No holiday, even for a day is worth that." The guard slid the plastic tray containing Julie's possessions across the table towards her. She gathered them together putting her jacket on as well as her shoes and her belt. Finally she returned her watch to her wrist.

"Is my friend free to go as well?" she asked the woman.

"Yes, my Supervisor said it was a mix up with him. Something to do with an injury he'd had years ago." Julie waited for further explanation as she didn't have a clue what she was talking about. None was offered so Julie went to the door. On the other side Leo was stood waiting for her, a big smile on his face. "Are we going to Malaga or what?"

Following the signs for gate 6, as instructed by the guard that had been questioning Leo, Julie turned to him and asked, "What was all that about? What injury, and why did they have to question you about it?" Leo brushed the question off with a mumbled answer, but then changed the subject.

"Why did they drag you off?" asked Leo. Julie didn't want him to worry that she no longer had the syringe so she altered the story slightly.

"They found my tablets in my rucksack and thought they were drugs. I showed them my appointment card and explained that they were part of my treatment and they accepted that." Leo wasn't sure whether to believe her or not, she was certainly in there for a long time to say it was such a short discussion. It was Julie's turn to change the conversation. "Come on, we will miss the plane if we don't hurry." She ran ahead before he could ask another question.

Once on the plane and in their allocated seats they had both turned their thoughts on to the day ahead. "How long does the flight take? "Asked Julie as the aircraft taxied out to the runway.

"About two and a half hours depending on wind speed and direction." Julie responded with a chuckle. "What are you laughing at?" Leo asked.

"Get you, pretending to know all about it. The real thing is a bit different to the arcade you know." Leo was a little hurt by the jibe. "Will you hold my hand while we take off?" asked Julie sliding her hand into his.

Clover House

"If anything goes wrong, holding my hand won't help you much," said Leo but he didn't complain, he held her hand and snuggled that bit closer to her.

During the flight Julie had her face pressed against the window for most of the time. She was fascinated how small everything looked from such a great height. She was forever pointing things out to Leo, who was trying to read the in-flight magazine.

"Can I get you anything to eat or drink?" asked the flight Attendant in a camp voice. He looked about nineteen years old, not so much as clean shaven, more the fact he wasn't old enough to grow facial hair yet.

"What do you have?" asked Leo. The young man offered Leo a menu showing all the options and said he would 'pop' back in a minute or two.

"Have you seen the bloody prices?" Leo said in a voice that could be heard by anyone within ten feet. The man in the seat in front turned around and lifted a bottle of coke. "I get mine in the airport, it's a lot cheaper." He then turned back.

Leo scanned the prices looking for the cheapest thing. He elbowed Julie to get her attention. "£2.61 for a bottle of water. It's water for Christ's sakes."

"Forget it," she said. "We'll get something when we get there." The flight attendant returned with his trolley. Before he could say anything Leo gave him the menu back with a dismissive shake of the head. The young man moved on.

Two hours and forty five minutes later the plane landed at Malaga airport. Julie had to be persuaded they weren't making a crash landing into the sea as they descended over the water on approach to the runway. As they exited the aircraft the July heat hit them both smack in the face. "It's so hot," Julie said as she made her way down the stairs. She nearly lost her footing as her eyes were eager to take in everything from the clear blue sky to the distant mountains that seemed to shimmer with the heat from the tarmac. She hurried the short distance from the plane's steps to the terminal. Once inside the air-conditioning made her feel chilly.

They followed all the other passengers through the system of showing passports and reclaiming luggage, even though they didn't have any. Coming through the last, glass doors they were welcomed by a multitude of people waving placards with names on. Julie was pushed to one side as a young girl shoved her way through and into the arms of what they presumed was her waiting boyfriend. Once again they followed the other passengers through the turnstile, across the concourse and into the revolving doors to outside. For the second time the

Clover House

heat hit them. "So where do we go now?" asked Julie.

"The beach of course. That's why we are here." Leo wiped the sweat from his brow.

"Where is it and how do we get there?" Julie pulled a baseball cap from her bag and placed it on her head, more to shelter her eyes from the sun than to protect her head.

"According to the maps I looked at it's not that far away. Plus the fact we flew over it just before we touched-down." Leo glanced around then saw what he was looking for. He grabbed Julie's hand and led her towards the taxi rank.

There was a queue but the line of taxis went on for as far as Leo could see, there must have been hundreds of them. Within a short time it was their turn. The white Mercedes edged forward and stopped. Julie jumped in one side and Leo walked round to the other door and got in besides her. He didn't sit next to the driver because he didn't want to start a conversation with him as he didn't know if he would be able to speak English or not.

"¿Dónde?" asked the driver looking into the rear view mirror at his new passengers. Leo presumed that he was asking for a destination. He didn't know any Spanish so simply replied with.

"To the beach, please." The driver slipped the car into first gear and started moving off slowly.

Clover House

He looked back into the mirror and asked in heavily accented English. "Any beach in particular?"

Leo shrugged his shoulders leant forward and said. "The nearest will be fine," then he added, "as long as it has palm trees on it." He smiled at Julie, she looked so excited. The driver smiled to himself, checked over his shoulder that the road was clear then put his foot down. The acceleration forced Leo back into his seat. It reminded him of the plane accelerating for take-off.

In less than ten minutes the Mercedes pulled up along the promenade of a beach that appeared to stretch out forever, the entire distance lined with palm trees waving in the breeze. The sea was an inviting bluish green, unlike the murky brown Leo remembered from a day trip to Bridlington some time ago.

"This looks great, here will do just fine." They gathered their things and got out of the car. Leo went to the driver's window to pay the fare. "How much is that?" Julie chuckled as Leo spoke slowly, announcing each word as though speaking to a lip reader.

"Ten euros," said the driver holding out his hand.

"Err euros?" asked Leo. Julie's chin sank to her chest.

Clover House

"Don't tell me you didn't change any money to euros?" Julie asked, not believing Leo could be so stupid and forgetful.

"Do you take pounds?" Leo asked the driver holding out a twenty pound note.

"Normally, no." The driver wasn't as stupid as Leo. He looked at the twenty pound note and knew that it was worth more than the fare. He also knew if he wanted to be paid anything for this trip then he would have to accept it. He reached out and snapped the note from Leo's hand and before he could object the driver said as he was driving away, "Obviously I have no pounds in change to offer you." Then he was gone. Julie shook her head and set off to the small gap in the wall that separated the beach from the promenade, Leo followed.

Feeling a little guilty, Julie turned to Leo and said "It doesn't really matter. We don't need anything else." She dropped her rucksack under the shade of a leaning palm tree, threw down her hat and ran to the sea. Feeling relieved in being forgiven so quickly Leo tossed his bag next to Julie's, pulled his t-shirt over his head and dropped that near the bags. He set off running after her as she approached the water's edge. Julie got soaked as Leo ran past splashing in the sea before taking a final plunge into an oncoming wave. "Leo you've still got your jeans

Clover House

on," Julie shouted as he surfaced, shaking his head to clear the water from his eyes and ears.

Leo smiled back, pointed to the sun and shouted "They'll dry in five minutes in this heat. Come in and join me." Julie had never felt comfortable with the sea but walked in up to her thighs.

Leo came towards her. "Don't fancy ticking number four off the list while we're here?"

"No I don't. My clothes are staying on thank you very much." Julie cupped her hands, scooped as much water as she could and threw it at Leo.

"Oh, like that is it Miss Sykes?" For the next fifteen minutes the water fight continued, ending up with Julie completely submerged. For some reason being alongside Leo made her fear of the sea disappear. At one stage she was trying to push him under the water, he was holding her waist close so if she succeeded, she too would go under. The struggling and the splashing died down until they were just stood, up to their waists in the sea looking at each other. Without saying a word their lips came together and for the first time since they had met they kissed passionately. A kiss neither of them would ever forget.

Back under the palm tree Julie turned to Leo and asked, "Are you nearly dry yet?"

Clover House

Leo who had been surprised how the frolicking in the waves had tired him out turned to face her and ran his hand over his trousers. "Nearly," he replied.

They both laid back and closed their eyes.

As they lay on the beach under the palm tree using their rucksacks as pillows, it wasn't long before they both drifted off into a deep sleep. Julie was having some weird kind of dream because she was letting out a muffled cry and shaking her head side to side. In the dream Julie was being chased by a very tall, dark monster, it didn't matter how fast she ran it was getting closer all the time.

Fortunately, like in most dreams just before you are caught you wake up; this is what happened to Julie. Unfortunately the dream didn't end when she opened her eyes. As she looked up the large, dark monster was standing over her, silhouetted against the bright sunshine. She let out a shrill cry that woke Leo up. He immediately sprang to his feet.

When Julie became fully conscious and placed her hand on her forehead to block out the sun's rays what she saw wasn't a monster at all. Leaning over her was the tallest black man she had ever seen wearing jeans and a Budweiser t-shirt. His hair was cropped short and his teeth were whiter than white.

Clover House

The man was taken aback by Julie's scream and when Leo jumped up he thought he was going to be attacked. He took several steps back and in a kind of reflex shouted out the words, "Asda price." All three of them stared at each other waiting for someone to make a move.

The black man, a beach seller, moved closer holding up an assortment of handbags, watches and sunglasses. "Asda price," he said again, obviously referring to the advert on TV by the well-known supermarket chain.

"Lucky, lucky, ten year guarantee," he said. Julie felt a little foolish and embarrassed and started trying to explain and apologise.

Getting any kind of reaction from a potential customer was a bonus, so to have one that is making conversation was an invitation to the seller to step forward and spread all his merchandise in front of them on a small red cloth brought for just such an occasion.

"I'm sorry I was dreaming," Julie explained to Leo. Leo accepted her apology and tried to explain to the man that he was wasting his time, they had no euros. As the conversation continued between Leo and the Beach seller Julie was picking various items from the display and examining them more closely.

"This is a Rolex," she said looking at one of the watches.

Clover House

"Just twenty euros ," said the black man.

Julie looked across at Leo and said, "These must be stolen or something. My father had a Rolex and it was worth hundreds, maybe thousands of pounds."

"Don't touch anything;" said Leo, "we don't want our finger prints on them."

Julie then lifted up a pair of sunglasses. "Look these are like my father's as well. Ray Bans cost an absolute fortune." She looked at Leo and using her hand to shield her mouth so the seller couldn't tell what she was saying, she said, "This lot must be worth a fortune." Leo didn't know the value of such things so he took Julie's word for it.

"Sunglasses twenty euros," said the seller.

"Looks like everything is twenty euros," said Leo, "that can't be right."

"We don't have any euros," Leo told him.

"What do you have if you don't have the euro?" The black man threw them a smile that almost dazzled them.

"We only have pounds I forgot to change my money before I came out," said Leo accepting responsibility for the mistake.

The man took a small calculator from his back pocket and punched some numbers in. "Watch fourteen, glasses fourteen. If you buy both you can have them for twenty pounds."

Clover House

Leo was trying to work out in his head what exchange rate he was using but gave up, he decided that if Julie was right and all these things were as expensive as she said they were, then they had to be a bargain. Leo's mind went back to the airport in the UK when they were stopped by Security. He didn't fancy going through that again, especially carrying stolen merchandise.

"No we're not interested," Leo announced. Julie was a little taken back. She wasn't used to anybody making her decisions for her, even Leo.

"Just a minute Leo," she said as she picked through various items on the cloth. She selected a pair of Aviator sunglasses. The seller took them out of her hand, opened them up and slipped them onto her head. Leo had to admit that they did suit her. Pulling a tiny mirror out of his back pocket the man hoping for his first sale of the day held it up so Julie could admire herself.

"I really don't think we should be talking to this man Julie. All this expensive stuff, he's clearly stolen it all." Julie wasn't listening, she was tilting her head this way and that looking at her reflection in the mirror.

"Julie!" Leo said a little louder this time, "I don't think we should be looking at these things." Julie slipped the glasses off and placed them back

Clover House

onto the cloth with the others. The seller completely ignored Leo and directed his sales pitch at Julie.

"We are not interested," said Leo firmly, but he might as well have been talking to a brick wall; this man could smell a sale at fifty yards.

Suddenly all hell broke loose and the man gathered his things together as quickly as possible, pushing them all into a large, canvas sack he carried on his back. In the distance Leo could see two policemen running down the beach in their direction.

Leo was convinced that at least one of the officers would stop and take their details but he was wrong, they both just kept running straight past them without giving them a second glance. It was obvious that they didn't have a cat in hell's chance of catching the beach seller. He must have been half their age, half their weight and twice as fit as the Spanish policemen.

As all three disappeared into the distance Leo turned to Julie. "That was a close call. I can just imagine Mr Jacobs's face if he'd got a call from the Spanish police to say that two of his residents have been arrested in Malaga with thousands of pounds of stolen goods. They both burst out laughing.

"Look," said Julie as she reached behind Leo and gathered something from the sand. "He must have dropped these." She was holding up the

Clover House

sunglasses she had been trying on only moments earlier.

"Well I guess they're yours now. I can't imagine him coming back for them," said Leo

"Shouldn't I give them to the police if they're stolen?" asked Julie.

Leo looked down the beach at the officers that had ran passed them, their bodies just a shimmer in the midday heat, and then they disappeared altogether. "Something tells me that they won't be returning either."

Pleased with her new acquisition Julie put the glasses on. "My very own Ray Bans." She posed like a model.

"I think you should take a rain check on that or at least before you start showing them off and bragging to everyone," Leo said.

"Why are they scratched?" she asked taking them off quickly to inspect them.

"No they're not scratched but the writing on the lens doesn't say Ray Bans, it says RAY BETIS! They're fake." He started laughing at the change of expression on her face.

"It's a good job that only you comes close enough to notice then, isn't it?" said Julie putting the glasses back on.

Clover House

"So when are you going to do what we came all this way for?" Julie wasn't sure what he was referring to. Then she remembered.

"I'm laid on the beach touching the shadow of a palm tree. This is what I came here to do. We can cross it off the list now." Julie laid her head back down.

"Excuse me. If we have come all this way I want a record of it." Julie sat back up not knowing what Leo was getting at. He turned around, opened his rucksack and started rummaging inside. Eventually he produced a camera.

"Where on earth did you get that?" Julie took it out of his hand and started examining it. "I didn't know you had a camera."

"Well it's not exactly mine," Leo confessed.

"Then who's is it?" she asked.

"It's Tommy Bishop's." Julie handed the camera back. "Please don't be like that. We will never get the chance to do anything like this again. I wanted you to be able to remember it." Julie knew Leo was right, this was a once in a life time adventure. Leo waited for a response.

"Okay. But when we've finished with it you return it," she said.

Leo jumped to his feet and checked that the sun was behind him. "Okay I want you touching the sand with your finger. It must be in the shade of the tree though." Julie knelt up and placed her forefinger on the beach whilst looking up, smiling towards the camera. Leo took several pictures, each one different, tilting the camera this way and that.

After returning the camera to his bag Leo glanced up and down the beach. "Fancy a walk? He asked Julie.

"Okay then." She gathered her things, threw the rucksack over her shoulder and started walking down to the water. Leo caught her up and held her hand as they walked. Once they got to the water's edge they turned and followed it walking towards the sun.

"Are you enjoying yourself?" asked Leo. Julie smiled up at him knowing he was fishing for a compliment.

"Who could not enjoy all this?" She half turned with her arm extended, "thank you Leo."

"What for?" he fished a little deeper.

"For all this, the concert, this trip, everything." Julie stopped walking and kissed him on the cheek.

"Oh my God," Leo just stood there with his mouth open. Julie frowned.

"It was just a kiss on the cheek Leo."

"Don't turn around now, Julie. Not unless you want to be mentally scared for the rest of your life." Leo let out a chuckle. Of course Julie wanted to see immediately what it was she wasn't supposed to be looking at. Leo held her shoulders so she couldn't turn. "Are you really sure you're prepared for this."

"I don't know until I see what it is." The anticipation was killing her. Leo released his grip and let his hands fall from her shoulders. Julie turned around slowly.

"Oh my God," she said, looking away without a second thought.

"I warned you," said Leo putting his hand over his mouth to stop him laughing out loud. About 50 feet behind them was an overweight man in his seventies doing star-jumps... in the nude.

"Look over there." Julie nodded over Leo's shoulder. He turned to find two woman playing bat and ball, also naked. "I think we may have strolled on to the nudist beach," she said.

"You never get people on a nudist beach that are young with fantastic bodies, do you?" This didn't stop Leo watching the women playing bat and ball for a little bit longer than necessary.

"I don't know I've never been to one before," said Julie taking a side step to try and block his view, unfortunately she was too short.

"No, neither have I," Leo corrected "But I bet I'm right." Julie changed direction and started walking back from where they'd come. "Are you just going to stand there staring?" Leo ran to catch her up but not without a couple of quick looks over his shoulder.

They spent the next hour strolling along the beach then up to where the bars and shops lined the promenade. Both of them were thirsty but knew they didn't have any euros to buy a drink. Most of the shops sold the same things, either toys to play on the beach with or souvenirs you wouldn't dare take home to loved ones. Leo looked at his watch. "I think we should start thinking about heading back to the airport."

"Do we have to? It's so beautiful here. Can't we just stay here forever?" Nobody wanted that more than Leo. He loved to see that carefree look on her face. To see her you wouldn't guess that she had a terminal illness. That they're time together was so limited. He closed the small gap between them and took her into his arms. Not only did he not want to leave, he didn't want to let her go either.

Rather than go through the same performance as last time with the taxi driver they agreed to walk back to the airport. Surely it couldn't be far. If they followed the road back then eventually they would come to where the taxi had originally dropped them off. Then it was just a simple case of going inland for ten minutes. The airport must be sign posted. So this is what they did.

Clover House

After strolling for thirty minutes, under a sun that felt like it was directly above them, they discussed the possibility that they had walked past the taxi drop off point. "We can't have past it, I remember a large fountain on the other side of the road and we haven't past that yet." Both of them were struggling with the heat, more so Julie. She had to sit down every fifty yards or so to have a rest and instead of the sun bringing some colour to her cheeks she was starting to look pale. "Do you need your medication?" asked Leo.

"I had a tablet when we started walking back. I think it's the heat." Julie tucked a strand of damp hair back under her cap.

"Do you want me to flag down a taxi?" without waiting for a reply Leo went to the side of the road and looked both ways. Julie didn't argue.

Fifteen minutes later Leo finally got the attention of a passing taxi by waving frantically and jumping up and down. As the driver pulled in Leo could see that it was the same driver that had taken them from the airport to the beach. The thought that ran through Leo's mind was, 'what was the bloody chance of that when he had seen hundreds of taxis at the airport.' As the driver stopped he recognised Leo and was just about to put his foot down and leave when Leo grabbed the car door, opened it and shouted, "I'll give you fifty pounds to take us to the airport." The driver smiled, applied the handbrake and nodded. Leo went to help Julie from her seat on the bench where she'd been resting, waiting for the taxi.

"But you don't have any euros." Even her voice sounded different now.

"Don't worry about that, it's sorted." Julie was so spaced out she didn't even realise it was the same driver as before. The driver tutted and shook his head thinking Julie had been drinking too much.

"She is not going to be the sick in my car, no?" Leo couldn't be bothered explaining so he just shook his head in response whilst getting Julie comfortable in the back. The driver wasn't convinced so he drove even quicker than he had before. The sharp curves and speed bumps did nothing to help Julie's condition. If Leo was honest with himself he would admit that Julie looked like she was going to throw up any minute.

Arriving at the airport terminal the taxi driver pulled up and jumped straight out of the car. Leo wondered where he was going. Suddenly the passenger door flew open and the driver reached in to help Julie out. He wasn't going to take any chances. He wanted her out of his car as soon as humanly possible. Leo paid the man and he got back inside the car and disappeared.

Clover House

"I think it maybe because I haven't had anything to eat or drink today. I'm not supposed to take my tablets on an empty stomach." It hadn't crossed Leo's mind that they had gone all day without any food or drink. euros or no euros he was going to get Julie something.

They walked into a small shop that sold magazines, sweets and a few snacks. Leo picked up a pack of chocolate biscuits and a can of lemonade. He checked over both shoulders to make sure nobody was watching then slid them both into his bag. From nowhere a security guard came around the end of the aisle and headed for Leo. Leaving Julie behind, he walked quickly in the other direction. He glanced back to see if the guard was following him. The next thing he knew he'd walked straight into a brick wall. It took Leo a couple of seconds to realise that it wasn't a wall he'd walked in to, it was in fact a large, Spanish policeman, gun and all. The guard shouted something and the policeman grabbed Leo by the arm. He was in serious trouble now.

Both the guard and the policeman started shouting at him. Behind the guard a new commotion was taking place. Julie had collapsed to the floor taking the whole shelf of soft drinks with her, cans and bottles were rolling across the shop floor, others smashed where they had landed. The policeman and guard forgot about Leo and rushed to Julie's side. Leo knew this was his opportunity to escape but he couldn't just leave her lying there. The policeman rolled Julie into a recovery position and lifted her eyelids, there was no response. Leo began to panic. The policeman was radioing for assistance and the guard helped the shop keeper lift the shelf back into position.

As Leo moved forward Julie, out of sight from the others, opened her eyes and winked at Leo. She had done all this as a distraction so he could escape. Taking his cue from her he walked unseen from the shop and across the passageway so he could watch from a safe distance.

Safely positioned behind a large pillar Leo looked on as the policeman sat Julie up and offered her a drink of water. She accepted, thanking him with a smile.

Eventually Julie stood up and apologised profusely to the shop keeper who waved off the gesture as he swept the debris into a corner. As she thanked everyone again Leo could see the policeman looking up and down the aisles, obviously searching for him.

"Julie. Over here," shouted Leo in an exaggerated whisper. Julie looked back at the shop to make sure nobody was watching then went over to join Leo. "Who's a clever girl then?" Leo asked.

Clover House

"Stop it you sound like a parrot." Julie did a double take in the direction of the shop. Although she was pretending to faint, the truth was she felt like she could do it for real at any moment. "I really need one of those chocolate biscuits Leo." He guided her down a corridor to a waiting area filled with seats. Leo retrieved the things from his bag and passed them to Julie. She dived into the biscuits like a starving animal.

It didn't take long for Julie to feel the benefit of something inside her stomach. She washed down the crumbs with a large gulp from the can of lemonade, swallowed and released the longest burp Leo had ever heard. They both rolled around laughing.

"I'll tell you something Leo French. Life is never boring with you around." She offered him the last biscuit.

"Admit it Miss Sykes, you wouldn't have it any other way." She smiled and nodded. He was right, since meeting Leo she had enjoyed the most fun she could ever recall having had.

Clover House
Chapter 12

The flight back was uneventful. In fact, Julie had slept most of the way. Leo looked down at her as she rested her head on his shoulder. She still looked unwell and he wondered if the whole day had been too much for her. As the captain announced they would be landing in fifteen minutes, Julie woke and stretched out. "Are we nearly back?" she asked as she was not fully awake during the call.

"Yes we'll be landing soon. We'll get a taxi back from the airport all the way to Clover House then you won't have to do anymore walking." Julie didn't argue. In fact she was quite relieved.

Unlike Malaga, Leeds Bradford airport didn't have an endless stream of taxis that you could just jump into. You had to go into a cabin, tell them where you wanted to go and pay for it there and then. Leo wasn't sure if this was to stop people doing a runner without paying or simply the fact that they didn't trust the drivers handling cash. Once they had been allocated a taxi they went outside to find it. Fortunately it pulled up to meet them just as they came out of the cabin. "I forgot how cold it was in England," said Julie as she pulled her jacket from her bag and struggled to put it on in the confines of the taxi.

Clover House

The driver overheard this comment and asked "Have you been away long?"

"Just since this morning," replied Leo. The driver thought he was trying to be funny so didn't continue the conversation.

As the taxi pulled up outside Clover House it began pouring down. Julie jumped out and using her rucksack to protect her hair from the rain she ran through the gate and up to the front door. Leo paid the driver and did likewise. As Leo reached for the door handle the door opened. Mr Jacobs stood blocking their entrance. "And where pray tell have you two been all day. You missed breakfast, lunch and dinner."

"I know Mr Jacobs," said Leo without any explanation, he then added, "Do you think Marge will make us a sandwich? We're starving." He tried to pass Mr Jacobs but he moved and blocked their way again.

"This isn't a hotel Leo. You can't just come and go without telling anybody where you're going." Mr Jacobs leaned in for a closer look. "Why are you both so red. It looks like sunburn."

Leo pushed his hand out from the porch into the falling rain. "In this weather Mr Jacobs, you must be joking." This time Leo and Julie successfully pushed passed him and made their way to the

Clover House

kitchen. Mr Jacobs smiled to himself as he watched them walk away.

"Is there any chance of a sandwich, Marge?" Leo shouted through the serving hatch, then without waiting for an answer he joined Julie at the dining table.

Marge appeared at the hatch. "It is not a hotel. You can't just come and go from my kitchen as it pleases you."

"So people keep telling me." He gave her one of his mischievous grins

She shook her head and added before disappearing. "I see what I can find."

"Well I think we can call today a success, don't you?" asked Leo.

"Yes. I really enjoyed myself but I think we have something to thank for getting us through those scrapes." Julie reached into her blouse pocket and pulled out the four leaf clover she'd taken from the garden that morning. At the same time Leo produced his lucky 50p piece. They put them next to each other on the table.

Leo put the clover on top of the coin. "I'm not sure which one it was but together we're invincible."

Marge brought out a couple of sandwiches, placed them between them with a jug of milk and two glasses. She muttered something then returned to the sanctuary of her kitchen. "Thanks Marge," Leo

Clover House

shouted after her, but she didn't reply, she just continued to mutter under her breath as the door closed behind her.

For the next week both Julie and Leo kept a low profile at Clover House. Leo wasn't sure if it was his imagination but he noticed both Mr Green and Mr Jacobs watching them and having discreet conversations. Julie needed the rest as well. She had looked peaky for a few days after their return. Miss Stevenson had made her go to the hospital with her for a check-up. This wasn't too bad as she had an appointment to go anyway.

Leo knew there was only one more thing on the wish list to do. He hadn't wasted anytime. He had been trawling through web sites for just what he needed and although it had taken all week he thought he had found just what he was looking for.

Julie was back to her old self. Her complexion had returned, unfortunately the suntan had only lasted a couple of days but the dark rings around her eyes had disappeared. Leo decided to leave the last thing on the list as a surprise. He didn't want Julie backing out of it.

Another week passed before Leo was ready and had completed all the ground work necessary.

Clover House

Whilst having lunch Leo turned to Julie and asked how she was, "I'm fine." She put her knife and fork down. "Why are you asking?"

"Fancy going out for a walk later?" he asked in a couldn't-care-less manner.

"Where to? You're up to something. I know that look." She picked up her utensils and continued eating, all the time watching him out of the corner of her eyes.

"Nowhere in particular. You haven't been out much lately and I think a walk will do you good. More chips?" He reached over for the bowl of chips in the centre of the table and offered them to Julie. She placed her hand over her plate preventing him adding to the pile that was already there. Maybe she was over reading in to what he was suggesting. She had been stuck in the house for some time and could do with a little, light exercise. Maybe a walk was just the thing.

"Okay. A walk sounds a good idea," she said.

"Right. We'll set off at 7pm, wrap up warm because it can still be a bit chilly when the sun goes down."

Her suspicions were aroused once again. Why the exact time of 7pm?"

Julie hadn't seen Leo for much of the afternoon. When she'd asked Mary (she refused to call her 'Fat Mary') if she'd seen him, she said he had gone out earlier. Julie sat with the others watching television. The only difference between her and the other house mates was that she was wearing her coat and shoes. She kept looking at her watch.

At 6:55pm Leo walked in the front door and straight into the lounge. "Are you ready to go?" he asked Julie. None of the others even looked away from the television. She stood up and asked, "Where have you been all afternoon?"

"I went to the arcade," Leo lied. "You know how cold it can get in that place. I didn't think you'd want to go. Sorry." Julie didn't believe him one bit.

They walked down the road and turned right at the T-junction. "Where are we going? We never go this way. In fact there isn't anything down here."

"I thought it would be a change." Leo linked her arm and guided her across the road. He could feel the rigidity in her arm. "Relax. We are only out for a stroll."

Another twenty minutes walking brought them to a part of Leeds that Julie didn't recognise. She pulled her arm free from Leo's and stopped walking. "Leo French you are up to something and unless you tell me what it is and where we are going, I'm not taking another step.

"You don't need to take another step. We have arrived." Leo's head tilted to look up at the sign above them. It read,

Clover House

Armley Sports Centre

Across the door there was another sign, it had been placed there by workmen, it read,

Closed for 2 weeks due to refurbishment

Julie read both signs twice. "Why on earth would you bring me to a sports centre, especially one that is closed?"

Leo grinned at her and said, "The swimming pool is still working."

"What do you mean the swim...?" The penny dropped. "Oh no, you can forget that." She started walking away. Leo ran after her and jumped in front to stop her going any further.

"Julie, you put it on the list and we agreed to do everything. You can't back out now," Leo pleaded.

"Yes, but, no, but, what if," she sighed. She knew he was right. "It's locked up, we can't even get in." She looked back at the locked doors and the sign over them.

"That's where I was this afternoon. Sorry I lied but needs must." They started walking back to the centre. "I found this place on the internet, they only closed it yesterday. The builders haven't even arrived

Clover House

yet. I came this afternoon to see if there was any other way in and guess what?"

"You found one," said Julie.

"Too right I found one. There is an entrance at the rear. I think it's a fire exit." Leo took Julie's hand and led her down the narrow passageway that ran down the side of the building. At the back was a large car park, the lights were still on but it was completely empty.

"What if they have security cameras?" asked Julie as her eyes scanned the car park and the back of the building.

"Again I've checked. There's none." Leo looked so pleased with himself. He went over to a door marked 'FIRE EXIT' and pulled the door. It opened without any resistance. He started to go inside when he was pulled back by Julie.

"They wouldn't leave that door unlocked. Did you do that this afternoon as well?" She was starting to have serious doubts about this.

"It only had a small chain across it. I didn't do much damage. Come on." He continued into the building. Julie followed reluctantly. It was difficult to see where they were going but it was obvious Leo had taken this route before. "Be careful there are some boxes on the floor down there, don't trip over them." Julie followed as closely as she could.

Clover House

"This door's a bit stiff." Julie watched while Leo grabbed the door handle with both hands and pulled with all his might. The door gave way. Stepping inside was like entering another world. The roof of the pool area was made of glass allowing the moonlight to flood in. The light shimmered across the swimming pool and reflected off the tiled walls surrounding the room.

"What do you think?" asked Leo, knowing she couldn't fail to be impressed. Julie threw her arms around his neck and planted a soft kiss on his lips.

"You've done it again Leo. Is there no end to your talents?" Again he held her hand and led her down the steps to the swimming pool. Julie walked to the far end of the room so she could look through the glass roof without the glare from the moon. She could see a million stars, each one seemed to flicker its own Morse code message. When she looked back towards Leo he was stood without his t-shirt on. She walked back to him.

"What are you doing?" she asked.

Leo looked confused. "I thought this is what you wanted. Number four on the wish list was to go skinny dipping. What better place could there be to do it than here?"

"I didn't say anything about doing it with anybody else." Leo looked like a small boy that had just lost his puppy. Julie moved closer to him and used her finger to lift his chin from his chest. "But then again Leo French I don't suppose you're just 'anybody'." Leo's face transformed immediately, his smile touched both ears. "I don't want you looking while I get undressed though." Just a touch of disappointment settled back on his face. "It's just that... I haven't got the best body in the world."

"And you think mine looks like Mr Universe?" They both laughed, releasing the tension.

They both started to take their clothes off slowly. Julie looked up to see Leo stood in his underpants as though he was waiting for her to catch up. A reflex action made her take a sharp breath that could be heard from the other side of the pool. She didn't realise she was doing it, but she'd froze, staring at his leg. Leo looked down at his thigh. The scar ran from his crotch to just above his knee. The flesh looked like it had been ripped open and sewn together by an amateur surgeon. Julie was aware that Leo had a limp, one that was more obvious on some days than others. He moved his hand to try and cover it.

"I'm sorry Leo, I didn't know." Do you want to talk about it?" Leo moved his hand away and looked at the scar.

"There's nothing to say really. It must have happened when I was very young because I don't even know how it happened." Julie had been

Clover House

hesitating, not wanting to know how Leo would react to her legs. She slid down her trousers and stood up straight. Both her thighs were badly swollen and blotchy.

"It's the injections I give myself. I try to do it in a different place every time to even out the damage, but it doesn't make any difference.

"Well aren't we the perfect pair." Leo slid down his pants and dived into the pool, but not before Julie confirmed the saying about black men. She followed his lead and finished taking off her trousers and pants. She slipped out of her bra and quickly dived into the pool. She surfaced just in front of Leo.

"They may have left the filter running but they sure as hell have turned off the heater in here." Leo laughed and started doing back crawl away from her.

"That's because you've been spoilt Miss Sykes. You're not swimming in the Mediterranean now." Julie chased after him doing the front crawl like a professional. When she caught up to him she tried to stand up, then realised they were in the deep end. Not thinking about Leo she put her arms around his shoulders to save herself. Misreading the signals Leo held her waist and pulled her in close.

"What do you think you're doing?" For a minute Leo regretted his actions and released her. Julie smiled at him and began swimming back to the

Clover House

shallow end. He took a deep breath and set off after her under the water. As he reached her he grabbed one of her legs, then surfaced. This time it was her turn to take the initiative. She held him close and kissed him. As he held her closer she could feel him pressing against her stomach.

"I think I need to get out," Julie said. Again Leo looked disappointed, wondering what he had done wrong. "It's not you, Leo." she kissed his cheek. "It's just that I'm fucking freezing." Leo laughed out loud. It was funny to hear Julie swearing, she hardly ever swore.

Leo was the first to reach the steps out of the pool. Julie watched him climb out and head over to a large cupboard in the corner. He opened the doors, reached in and pulled out a pile of towels. He wrapped one around his waist, spread half a dozen on the floor then carried one over to the steps so he could wrap it around her as she got out.

After drying themselves they used clean towels to keep themselves warm, none of them suggested getting dressed yet. They just sat on the towels he'd spread out each wearing a large bath sheet over their shoulders. Using hers like a bed sheet Julie laid back and looked through the glass roof at the stars. The moon had moved on so that each star was shining even brighter. Leo joined her.

"Which one is yours?" he asked.

Clover House

"Are you taking the Mick?" asked Julie without looking at him.

"I'm being serious. You said you are going to live on a star I just wondered if you'd picked one yet."

"I don't think it works like that. You just get the next available one, but just so you know where to look I'll have a big neon sign that reads JULIE'S PLACE," replied Julie. She then asked, "In the future will you look up and think of me?"

Leo was beginning to regret bringing up the subject. A lump came to his throat. "I will lie on my blanket, just like this, looking up at the stars every night." Julie turned onto her side and put her arm across his chest.

"And I will be looking down on you all the time. So you better behave Mr French." She tickled him playfully under the arm. Leo began tickling her back. They rolled this way and that both trying to get the advantage, it ended with Leo on top holding Julie's arms by her side. Again she felt him pressing against her stomach. She slid her arms free and cupped them behind his neck, pulling him down until their lips met.

She looked at the night sky over his shoulder and for the next thirty minutes gave herself to him body and soul.

Clover House

Leo opened his eyes. Julie was lying on his shoulder, her breathing, louder than normal told him she was asleep. A noise in the distance had woken him. He sat up laying Julie's head down gently. Suddenly the door burst open and a couple of people ran down the steps towards them, lights from their torches blinding him. "Don't move," shouted a man's voice. Now Julie was awake as well. They grabbed towels and put them around themselves before standing. The two policemen lowered their torches and ordered them to get dressed.

"Don't I know you?" one of them asked Leo.

"I don't think so," said Leo trying to put his pants back on without the towel falling down.

"I remember, Clover House." The policeman seemed a little embarrassed. "It was me and my partner that brought you the sad news about your mother. What are you doing here?" The policeman looked around at the towels spread on the floor.

"Just fulfilling a wish officer." The policeman flashed his torch onto Julie who was just finishing putting on her bra.

"Sorry madam." He dropped the torch beam immediately. "You do realise we are going to have to take you both to the station?"

"Can't you give us a break? Maybe even a lift back to Clover House?" asked Leo. He knew he was

Clover House

pushing his luck. The two policemen looked at each other one gave a nod to the other.

"Well taking into consideration how we last met, and the fact that no criminal damage has been done, I suppose we may be able to be a bit more lenient than normal. We'll take you back to Clover House but we will have to come in and explain to the Manager where we found you." Leo presumed they didn't see the broken chain on the fire door at the rear.

Driving back in the police car Leo turned to Julie and asked, "Do you have your four leaf clover with you?"

"No, why?" she frowned thinking it was an unusual question given the circumstances.

"That proves it then. It's my lucky 50p piece that brings us all the good luck." Leo held up the coin.

"Then why are we sat in a police car?" she asked.

Clover House
Chapter 13

Arriving back at the home the police car pulled up and out got the two officers. Leo and Julie had to wait for them to open the doors as they only opened from the outside. Looking up Leo saw Mr Jacobs stood with his arms crossed in the doorway. Unbeknown to them one of the officers had rang ahead and explained the situation. The officers escorted them to the gate.

"It's okay officers I'll take it from here. Thank you very much," said Mr Jacobs. The officers acknowledged him with a nod and returned to their car.

"What on earth do you two think you were doing?" Mr Jacobs asked, aiming the question at Julie. Leo tried to brush past him but he stood his ground. I have told you before Leo, this is not a hotel. We have a duty of care for the two of you and you're making our job very difficult.

Julie spoke for them both. "We are very sorry Mr Jacobs. I can promise that it won't happen again."

"I just don't know what's gotten into you two. You never used to behave like this. If necessary I will introduce a curfew for both of you. I don't want to but I won't allow the police having to come here again." He moved to one side and let them both pass. They held hands and walked towards the

Clover House

kitchen. Mr Jacobs couldn't help smiling. He knew what had come over them.

Marge had left for the day and looking back Leo saw Mr Jacobs going up the stairs back to bed. "You ready for bed?" Leo asked. Julie shot him a rueful look.

"No I didn't mean that." Leo flushed. "I meant are you tired yet? I'm not, in fact I'm hungry. Fancy something to eat?"

Julie pulled out a chair and sat at the table. "That would be nice."

Ten minutes later Leo appeared carrying a tray. He placed it on the table and passed Julie a plate containing two slices of toast along with a cup of tea. She did what she always does when eating bread at meal times; she nibbled all the crust off first. Leo smiled. "What's so funny?" she asked.

"Nothing, I think you're funny." Julie frowned. "I mean funny cute, not funny peculiar." She smiled back.

Leo swallowed the piece of toast he'd been chewing. "Well I must admit I never thought we'd pull off all five wishes on the list. Not in a million years."

"We didn't." replied Julie sitting back and taking a gulp of her tea. Leo put his cup down and sat up straight. His lips moved as he counted the fingers on his left hand. Then he did it again to make sure he hadn't made a mistake.

"We have, we completed all five." He looked at Julie waiting for an explanation.

"We did six." she said as one side of her mouth went up into a lopsided smile. Leo started counting his fingers again. After getting to five he thought for a while before it dawned on him. He smiled as well.

"Ah, I see. That was the one you wouldn't tell me about." Julie replied with a larger smile and a wink.

The atmosphere was shattered when the door flew open and in walked Fat Mary. "Can I smell toast?" she asked following her nose and looking down at the empty plates on the table.

"Help yourself," said Leo nodding towards the kitchen door. "I've left the bread out." Mary walked passed them and straight into the kitchen. Leo shouted after her. "Be careful with the toaster the on/off button doesn't work. You have to plug it in then unplug it when you've finished."

"I'm kind of tired. Do you mind if I go to bed?" Julie asked Leo.

"I'll come up with you. I'm beat as well." They cleared away their pots and climbed the stairs together. Outside Julie's room Leo kissed her cheek and said goodnight. She watched him walk down the corridor before entering her room. It was another

Clover House

hour before Leo got to sleep. He just kept re-running the day through his head.

"FIRE, FIRE! Everybody out!" At first Leo thought he was having a nightmare. It wasn't until he opened his eyes and felt Mr Jacobs shaking him violently that he realised it was very real. There was a distinct smell of smoke. "Come on Leo don't waste time getting your things, just go straight downstairs and get outside. The fire engine is on its way." Then just as quickly Mr Jacobs left his bedroom and ran on to the next one along the corridor. Leo could hear him kicking the door down, presumably it had been locked.

Leo jumped out of bed. His first thought was to make sure Julie was okay. He grabbed his jeans and pulled them on. As he entered the corridor the smell of smoke was much stronger. He could see the smoke coming up the staircase.

He ran down the corridor to Julie's room. The door was ajar. He pushed it open, the bed was empty. She must be outside already. Leo took the stairs three at a time jumping the last five in one go. Looking to his left he could now see the flames licking the walls of the dining room. The front door was open so he was just about to run straight outside when he heard an unfamiliar voice at the top of the steps behind him. The person was calling for

Clover House

help. Leo had to make a choice: the safety of outside or to go back upstairs to help the person calling for help. In his mind there wasn't a choice to make, he turned and ran back up the stairs. At the top he found the twins, one was laid passed out on the floor the other trying to pick up his brother. "You get the feet," said Leo. Between them they carried the limp body down the stairs and outside into the fresh air. Once outside the unconscious brother started to come around.

"Thank you Leo." That was the first word either twin had ever said to another resident. That was also the reason Leo hadn't recognised the voice calling, he'd never heard it before.

Across the road, gathered together were most of the other residents in various stage of dress. Some of the neighbours had also come out of their homes to see what the commotion was. In the distance Leo could hear the sirens of the fire engine.

His adrenaline had taken over. Leo could feel his own heart thumping. He must have inhaled some fumes when coming down the stairs as his throat itched and he struggled to breathe. He coughed several times to try and clear his lungs. Looking back towards the building he saw Johnny Fish running out of the front door. He collapsed onto the grass struggling to breathe. One of the neighbours ran across and helped him away from the building. Next

Clover House

to appear was Mr Jacobs carrying Wee Willy. He too fell to his knees on the lawn, again the neighbour that helped Fish returned to help Mr Jacobs.

The fire engine pulled up and everybody was told to stand further back. Leo started looking around the crowd for Julie. After searching for five minutes he began to panic. An ambulance arrived and started accessing casualties. Mr Jacobs was having a problem catching his breath so was immediately put onto oxygen. Leo looked again at all the faces in the crowd, he couldn't see Julie's. He ran up to Fat Mary. "Mary have you seen Julie?" She was crying and didn't seem to be listening to him. He repeated the question but got no response. He moved on and started shouting Julie's name out.

Another ten minutes had passed when Leo turned and looked at the flames now climbing the curtains inside the house. He ran over to where Mr Jacobs was getting attention at the rear of the ambulance. "Mr Jacobs did you see Julie come out?" A paramedic tried to move Leo away but he refused to budge. Mr Jacobs lifted the mask off his face and in a voice that was hardly legible, croaked the words, "Not in her bedroom." Leo looked back at what was Julie's bedroom window. Black smoke billowed out.

Leo ran up to the fireman that was wearing the white helmet, he was the one giving out orders and

Clover House

instructions to the others. "I think there is still someone inside."

The fireman looked up from his clipboard and asked, "Who, and why do you think that?"

"She's called Julie Sykes. I just spoke to Mr Jacobs who evacuated us all and he said he didn't see her. I've been looking around and she's not out here."

"Have you any idea where she might be in the building?" asked the fireman.

Leo started to cry. "I don't know. She could be anywhere." The fireman called over one of his colleagues who was kitted out in breathing apparatus. He shouted instructions into his ear and slapped him on the back. He then wrote something on to the clipboard as the other fireman ran towards the building. Leo fell to his knees sobbing.

Word went around the crowd that there maybe someone still inside building. The anguish was tangible. There was a brief moment of moans and discussion before everybody fell silent, waiting for the fireman to return.

After an eternity you could see movement near the door. Then there was a small explosion that made the onlookers shield their faces. When they looked back the fireman was coming out of the front door, he was carrying something. At first the bundle in his arms resembled a rolled up carpet. He laid it down on the lawn and started unravelling it. The crowd gasped. It was a person.

Leo ran forward. The fireman wearing the white helmet tried to stop him but he didn't stand a chance. Leo pushed away his arms and continued running to where Julie was laying. Close behind Leo was a paramedic. Julie's face was black with soot. She wasn't moving. The oxygen mask was placed over Julie's face whilst the paramedic checked her for other injuries. He lifted one eye lid and shined a torch into her face then he did the same with the other. No response.

"Don't do this to me Julie. Don't you fucking dare leave me now." Leo's initial fear had turned to anger. He fell to his knees at her side. The paramedic had to shove him out of his way so he could get in position to start resuscitation. He knelt by her side and placed one hand on her chest then the other hand on top of that one, with his arms outstretched he started pumping a regular rhythm. The fireman who brought Julie out tried to pull Leo away but he wouldn't move.

Just when the paramedic was thinking of stopping Julie suddenly gasped, pulled away the oxygen mask and threw up, all over his trousers. "Jim, get the stretcher over here." He shouted to the other paramedic that was dealing with Mr Jacobs. Within seconds they had lifted Julie on to the gurney

Clover House

and were wheeling it towards the ambulance at speed. As it hit the back bumper of the ambulance the wheels folded up automatically and it slid into the back.

Mr Jacobs was already in the ambulance, the oxygen mask once again over his face. Leo tried to climb in the back but one of the paramedics pulled him back.

"Sorry there's no room. We are taking them to Leeds General Infirmary if you want to follow." Leo didn't have any transport. He watched on as the paramedics climbed aboard, started the engine, turned on the blue lights and siren, and then disappeared down the road.

Some of the neighbours had taken in the residents of Clover House whilst other accommodation could be found. Leo was sat in the dining room of one such neighbour receiving sympathy and offers of tea every five minutes. He stared across the room at Fat Mary who refused to meet his glare. She was still crying. Leo hated every fibre of her body. He knew who was responsible for all this.

It was two hours later when Mrs Westland turned up in a minibus and rounded them all up. She wasn't happy that her sleep had been disturbed, and let everybody know it. "Come on everyone get inside." She shouted. Each of the residents paused

Clover House

and looked back at the home before getting on to the bus. The firemen were still dowsing the building with water. In addition to the first fire engine another one had arrived with a long extendable ladder. On the top a fireman controlled a hose that swung backwards and forwards spraying the roof with gallons of water.

Leo asked Mrs Westland if he could go to the hospital to be with Julie. She shrugged the request away like an annoying fly. Once everybody was seated Mrs Westland stood at the front of the bus and demanded silence.

"We have found alternative accommodation for all of you, though not in the same establishment. We are going to have to spread you all over three different homes. Some will be more permanent than others." When she finished she turned around and sat down in the driving seat. There were hundreds of questions being fired at her from 'when can we get our things?' to 'who will be placed together?' She ignored each and every one of them.

They pulled up outside a large building that looked very similar to Clover House. Mrs Westland produced a sheet of paper and called a few names out. Each person called moved to the front of the bus and got off. An elderly man greeted them with a smile and ushered them inside.

Clover House

At the next stop Mrs Westland did the same thing. Only this time she called everyone else's name except Leo's and Johnny Fish's. The two of them watched through the window as once again the residents were warmly welcomed. This time three members of staff escorted them into the building after wrapping a blanket around their shivering bodies. Leo watched as Fat Mary walked away from the bus, still crying.

After a short drive the minibus pulled up outside a modern looking building on the opposite side of Leeds. "Right you two this is your stop."

"Mrs Westland, when can I visit Julie at the hospital?" asked Leo as he stepped off the bus, he was worried sick.

"You'll have to ask the Manager here. Good luck with that." She closed the automatic doors but not before she'd let out a chuckle.

There was nobody waiting for them like the other homes. "Guess we drew the short straw," said Fish ringing the bell on the door. Eventually the door opened a little and a woman's head poked around.

"Ah, you must be the two from Clover House. Well don't just stand there, come inside."

Leo and Fish entered the building and looked around. "Don't get too comfortable, I don't think you'll be staying long. Follow me." The woman led

Clover House

the way down the corridor and up the stairs. All the rooms were numbered with silver digits.

"I was wondering when I could go and see my friend that was taken to hospital?" The woman froze, she then turned slowly.

"Let's get one thing straight. I don't know how your last place was run but I think you may find things a little different here. This is most definitely not a hotel. If you want to leave the building you must be signed out by a member of staff, and signed back in again. That is if you have a legitimate reason to leave in the first place. Nobody goes out after 7pm or before 8am. All meals will be taken in the dining room, no food in the rooms." The woman who they later found out was called Miss Bailey, spent the next twenty minutes listing the Do's and Don'ts applicable to the home. "...and finally. With regards visiting your friend in hospital, we do not run a taxi service so any costs incurred for such a journey will be met from your own expenses. Do you have any questions?"

Without waiting for a reply she turned and using a card key she unlocked the room numbered 112. She stepped inside and turned on the light and offered the card to Leo. "Don't lose this or you will pay for the replacement." Without another word she walked out of the door and closed it behind her.

Clover House

"I guess we are sharing," said Fish. Leo darted across the room and jumped on to the bottom of the bunk beds. Fish smiled. "I prefer the top anyway." They both laughed out loud.

Leo didn't get any sleep that night. He was too worried about Julie. He woke up and looked around the sterile bedroom and wondered what else could go wrong. "You asleep?" asked a voice from above.

"No," answered Leo. "Want to go and get some breakfast and do a bit of exploring?" He replied.

"Sounds like a plan," said Fish jumping down from the bed above and going over to look out of the window. "You have any idea where we are?"

"No. We were driving for a while so I'm guessing we are on the other side of Leeds. You recognise anything out of the window?"

"Not a thing." said Fish.

Leo used the bunk above to pull himself out of bed and went to join Fish at the window. He gathered his clothes from the floor and held them to his nose. "I think the first thing we need to do is get ourselves some new clothes, these stink."

Going down the stairs they asked another resident where they could find the dining room, the person walked by completely ignoring the question. The second person they encountered pointed down the corridor and said nothing. "These are a sociable

Clover House

bunch," Leo said to Fish. They started walking down the corridor when Fish stopped and called Leo back. "What is it?" he asked.

Fish nodded towards the door to his left, the sign read 'Manager'. "Shall we ask about getting some new clothes?" Without waiting for an answer he knocked on the door.

"Come in." They opened the door and stepped inside. A middle aged man wearing a bowtie stood up from his desk. "Ah the newcomers, come in. God your clothes smell. We'll have to do something about that." Leo smiled. This man seemed much more amiable than the woman last night.

"Actually that's why we came to see you," Leo said then added, "My friend was taken to hospital during the fire. I was wondering if it would be possible to find out how she is doing."

"I can answer that now," said the Manager. "It was all over the news this morning." Then he added as an afterthought, "She's doing alright." This was the best news Leo could have hoped for.

After hearing all the rules read out last night he had feared that visiting the hospital would have been outlawed. Although he knew he'd be pushing his luck, he asked anyway. "Would it be possible to go and visit her?"

"I don't see why not. Do you know your way around Leeds? Do you need someone to go with

Clover House

you? Do you have the bus fare?" All these questions seemed to come at once and in Leo's opinion they all sounded a bit stupid, as though he were talking to an idiot.

"Err, yes, no and yes."

"The Manager had to think about the questions he'd asked to work out the answers, "right, good, fine. You seem like a sensible man. If anybody asks, tell them I gave you permission to go."

Leo and Fish thanked the Manager and started leaving the office when he called to them, "do have your breakfast first though. Never do anything on an empty stomach." Leo decided there and then that he liked this man. He thought he was a little wacky, maybe even eccentric, but beyond that he reminded Leo of Mr Jacobs, someone you could describe as fair.

An eerie silence hung in the air of the dining room. Leo guessed that there must have been approximately twenty residents all sat eating their breakfast without saying a word. Then he saw why. At the head of the table was the woman who had greeted them on their arrival. Not speaking during breakfast was obviously a rule.

She watched them hovering by the door, her spoon poised a centimetre from her mouth, waiting to see what they did. Fish followed Leo over to the

Clover House

table. They selected two vacant seats as far away from the woman as possible.

"Not there," she bellowed across the room, "here." She used her spoon to point at two empty seats either side of her. They walked slowly, aware that the rest of the residents were watching them. At the same time both Leo and Fish pulled out the seats, settled into them and pulled them back under the table.

"This is not the Savoy gentlemen. If you are expecting a waitress you will be waiting for a very long time." Looking around they spotted a long table with various cereals along with toast and soft drinks against the back wall. They walked towards the table trying to stifle the giggles that were building at the back of their throats.

After pouring out two bowls of cornflakes Fish turned to Leo, "would Sir be requiring the milk?" They both burst out laughing, much to the annoyance of the woman watching them at the head of the table. They returned to their seats and like the rest of the diners, ate their breakfast without a word.

Clover House
Chapter 14

Leo had asked Fish if he had wanted to accompany him to the hospital. For some reason he felt responsible for him. Fish had declined saying that he would rather explore the home, plus the fact he said hospitals give him the creeps.

After going back to the Manager and asking him which bus he needed and directions to the bus stop, Leo had changed into some fresh clothes (supplied by the home) and set off as quickly as he could. Never having arrived into Leeds from this direction he wasn't surprised when he missed his stop. He didn't really mind the extra distance he had to walk but it did delay him and according to the Manager at the home, visiting times at the hospital were restricted.

Arriving at the hospital, he approached the lady on reception and asked where he might find Julie Sykes. Her reply of, "what ward is she on?" seemed a little stupid, if he'd known that he would have gone straight there and avoided this conversation. He waited while she looked on the computer and made several phone calls. "She is on ward J10," she eventually announced. After getting directions and thanking her he went to go and find it as quickly as possible.

Clover House

He entered the double doors labelled J10 to find a series of smaller wards each containing just four or five beds. Going between these he peeped inside trying to be as unobtrusive as possible. In the last one he recognised Mr Jacobs but not the other three people sat around Julie's bed. Julie was sat up listening to her visitors speak amongst themselves. As he entered it appeared the other visitors had decided to leave so Leo stood back while hands were shaken and goodbyes were said. He smiled and nodded to them as they all passed each other at the end of Julie's bed.

Seeing Leo, Julie ripped off the mask she was wearing to help her breathe. She tried to say something but only a croak made its way out of her mouth. Mr Jacobs jumped up and made her replace the mask. "You've been told not to try and talk Julie." Her smile appeared either side of the mask.

"Who was that?" Leo asked looking over his shoulder as the previous visitors left the ward.

"Family," replied Mr Jacobs without adding any further explanation. Leo frowned, trying to recall any family Julie may have mentioned, without success. "How's the new home Leo?" Was it his imagination or was Mr Jacobs trying to change the subject.

"It's okay. The Manager is quite chatty but there's a woman who's..."

Clover House

"That will be Miss Bailey. I've heard a lot about her. Ex-military I understand."

"Ex-military? Where? Colditz?" Leo laughed at his own joke. Then it was his turn to change the subject. "How's this wounded soldier? Come to that how are you Mr Jacobs? You looked in a bad way the last time I saw you."

"I've just been discharged. They told me to get a lot of fresh air over the next few days. Typical NHS using fresh air as medication now. They say anything to save on the budgets."

Julie held Leo's hand. It was killing her not being able to talk. He leant forward and kissed her forehead. "What have they said about Julie?" Leo felt uncomfortable discussing her without her being able to contribute to the conversation but he had to know.

"She just needs rest. She inhaled a lot of smoke. She was lucky really." Mr Jacobs stood up and offered his chair to Leo. "I must get back. There is a lot to sort out at Clover House."

Leo hesitated before asking the question, as he knew how much the home meant to this dedicated Manager. "How is it? Is it repairable?"

"Fortunately it's not as bad as we all first thought. Most of it is just smoke damage and it was insured so it's just a case of waiting for the work to be done." Mr Jacobs answered the question he knew

Clover House

was on Leo's lips, "then we can all go back to how we were." Julie squeezed Leo's hand.

After Mr Jacobs left, the conversation was all one way. Leo told Julie about the fire and his theory about how it started. How he had raised the alarm when he couldn't find her in the crowd outside. About the fireman that rushed back into the burning building to save her. He then explained that all the residents had been split up. When he told her about the woman at his new home and what happened at breakfast Julie started laughing and it sent her into a coughing fit. This made Leo feel guilty and he vowed to himself to keep things on a serious note in future, well until she was at least fit enough to laugh.

He was curious though as to why she wasn't in her bedroom when the fire started. Julie pointed to a pad and pen on the bedside cabinet. Leo reached over and gave it to her. She scrawled the following sentence

Couldn't sleep so went downstairs to watch TV
Fell asleep.

That explained everything.

Leo visited Julie everyday that week. On his third day she wasn't wearing the mask anymore but was still under strict orders not to speak. For some

Clover House

people this one sided way of conversing would be quite awkward but for Julie and Leo there was no such difficulty. Leo had wrapped the nurses around his finger so when most people left at the end of visiting time Leo was allowed to stay on as long as he wanted. Though he knew he had to be back before the curfew was imposed, he didn't want to give them an excuse to end his visits.

Arriving back at the home he was just in time for dinner so went straight through into the dining room. He was relieved to see that there were no members of staff seated at the table, especially 'that' woman. He was also surprised to see that Johnny Fish was absent as well but assumed he must have a good reason.

After finishing his meal he sneaked a couple of buns from the table, just in case Fish hadn't had anything to eat. What he didn't expect to find when he returned to their room was Fish laid in his bed. He crept quietly up to the bunks, not knowing if he was asleep or not. As he got closer he could hear him whimpering. "Fish, you okay?"

"Just leave me alone," he replied between sobs and pulling the covers that little higher.

"What's wrong? Has something happened?" Leo asked.

"Just leave me alone." Leo didn't know if he was the cause of Fish's upset.

Clover House

"I'm not going anywhere until you tell me what's happened." Fish slowly turned over. His face was tear stained but what Leo hadn't expected was the welt mark down the side of his face. "Who the fuck has done that?" Leo knew that in a place like this there was always going to be that element of violence. Tommy Bishop had been the proof of that.

Fish eventually managed to gain his composure. He jumped down from his bed and went over to the window. Leo thought Fish needed an excuse not to look at him whilst relaying the story. "You know that guy who works in the kitchen?"

The only person Leo could recall seeing in the kitchen looked about twenty years old with a sullen face. He didn't want to interrupt Fish's flow so just answered yes.

"I was one of the first down for dinner, so I was just hanging around. I saw someone rushing out of the kitchen, she looked so upset, so I decided to go and find out what had caused her to be so distressed." When I went in that guy, appeared from nowhere and forced my arm up my back, he really hurt. Then he started calling me names. When he released me I thought that was it, but as I started walking away he kicked me in the back of my knees. I fell down really hard." The memory of it made his bottom lip shiver.

Clover House

Leo was confused. "Why would anyone do that?"

Fish continued, "He said that after dinner I had to go back to the kitchen and help tidy things away. He said he doesn't get paid enough to clear up after people like me. I don't want to go back Leo." If it was one thing that Leo couldn't stand it was a bully. Just listening to Fish telling the story made his blood boil.

"We'll go and see the Manager, Johnny. He'll put a stop to all this." Leo started towards the door.

"No, no. We can't Leo. He warned me that if I tell anyone he'll just deny it and they'll believe him over me as his mother is the Deputy Manager." Fish stood in between Leo and the door blocking his path.

"We can't just let this go. What will happen when you don't turn up?"

"I'll have to go," said Fish as his sobs returned.

Leo had an idea. He was probably right. They may believe this guy over them as they are new to the home, and they didn't have any proof. "I'll go and see him. I'll tell him you are ill." Before Fish could object Leo pushed passed him and went through the door. As he walked down the corridor he was trying to work out a solution to this problem, without much luck

All the diners had left so Leo walked straight over to the kitchen door and entered. "Well what do we have here?" Asked the twenty year old Leo had

Clover House

seen previously. He presumed this was the man Fish had been talking about.

"I understand you have been hassling my friend," Leo said pushing his chest out and trying to make himself look as tall as possible."

"I wouldn't call it that. We had a discussion and he offered to help me out in the kitchen." The man picked up a carving knife and made his way towards Leo. "Where is he anyway, he was supposed to be here helping me clear this lot away."

Leo stood his ground. "He won't be coming down..." Before he could finish his sentence the man grabbed him and spun him around. Like Fish, his arm was forced up his back, he couldn't move. The carving knife was inches from his cheek.

"If he's not coming down then you'll have to help." Leo had heard about people like him. Working in homes and treating the residents like dirt. He wasn't sure what to do. He could see why Fish was so shook up.

"Okay, okay. I'll help, but let me go you're hurting me. You're going to break my arm." Leo stopped struggling, it only made the pain worse.

"That would be a shame. They do say kitchens are a dangerous place, and you shouldn't be in here anyway, so in theory it would be your own fault." The man let Leo go but stood close in case he made a run for it. "In fact congratulations, you can consider

Clover House

yourself my new permanent helper. After every meal I want you in here cleaning up. If anybody asks, you're volunteering. In fact you can start straight away."

Leo had to think quickly. "Okay, but can I go and change my clothes first?" The man looked at him suspiciously. He'd worked over half the residents in the home and never before had any of them been so submissive so quickly.

"Okay you can go and get changed but you better come straight back here. If I hear you've blabbed to anyone or you don't come back, both you and your little buddy will regret it." He slid his finger down the point of the blade to emphasise the point.

Leo ran back to his room as quickly as his bad leg would let him. Fish was waiting for him, clearly relieved that he had returned at all. "What happened?" He asked. Leo sat on the edge of the bed to get his breath back and compose himself.

"You were right Fish. That man is dangerous and needs dealing with.

Fish watched on as Leo got changed. Without any explanation he then started routing through the box of belongings that had come from Clover House that morning. Everything smelt of smoke. "Here it is," he said as he pulled out his rucksack. He undid the draw string and plunged his hand in up to his elbow.

Clover House

Like a magician producing a rabbit, Leo withdrew his hand, only he was holding a camera.

"What are you going to do with that?" asked Fish.

"That guy is probably right. No one would take our word on face value. We need proof." He held the camera up as though it was the lost Holy Grail.

Leo returned to the kitchen, much to the surprise of the man that had threatened him. "Here he is my little black helper," he said thinking he had struck gold with this resident. He walked over to the sink and started piling up all the pots from dinner. What he didn't see was Leo taking the camera out of his pocket, setting it to video mode, pushing the record button and placing it on top of the fridge. "I want all these cleaning and stacking up over there on that table." Leo glanced at the camera to make sure he was in shot.

"How much am I getting paid for this?" Leo asked.

The man stormed over. "Are you fucking winding me up?" He pushed Leo back hard against the work surface. He doubled over with pain as the edging caught him right in the kidneys. Leo stood up and moved back in front of the camera.

Clover House

"I take it that means its minimum wage then." He even managed to smirk at his own joke through the pain. He braced himself for the next onslaught.

"Ladies and gentleman we have a comedian in our midst," said the man as though he were addressing an audience. "Laugh at this." He brought his knee up and 'dead-legged' Leo right on his bad thigh. He crumpled to the floor cursing under his breath. The next kick hit him square in the stomach.

The man bent down and whispered into Leo's ear, "If that lot isn't sorted by the time I get back then I'll really give you something to laugh at. Leo stayed on the floor until he was sure the man had gone. He didn't know how much time he had so he struggled to his feet and over to the fridge. He used the work surfaces to help support his weight as he moved.

Reaching up for the camera created its own problem. As he stretched it caused a sharp pain down his right side. He knew that it would be worth it, he'd already decided to show the film to Mr Jacobs rather than anybody else at this home. He didn't want his evidence accidently disappearing.

He turned the camera over so he could play back what he had captured. The screen was blank so he pushed the on/off button several times.

Nothing.

Clover House

It had all been a waste of time because the battery had died. He was about to throw the camera at the wall when he remembered that it still contained the pictures of Julie, "What would you do in this position, Julie?" He'd directed his question at the camera as though she was actually inside the small plastic box.

He wasn't sure where the idea came from but looking around the kitchen he saw just what he needed. It was going to be dangerous but he had no alternative. Desperate times called for desperate measures.

He found the largest pan in the kitchen and filled it with several bottles of cooking oil. He positioned the pan on one of the burners at the back of the oven and started looking for the cutlery drawer. Once he'd found it he pulled out several knives before finding the exact one for the job. Returning to the pan he started loosening two of the screws that held the handle in place. He stood back admiring his handy work. He lit the burner, returned the knife to its drawer and casually wondered out of the kitchen and back to his room.

Fish asked what had happened but Leo said nothing and simply climbed into his bed to rest the injuries he'd sustained.

The kitchen worker returned carrying a large sack of potatoes. He looked around the room and

Clover House

wasn't too surprised to see it empty. "Maybe I was wrong. This one may need a little more breaking-in than I expected."

Suddenly the smell of burning oil hit him. He instinctively looked over at the stove. He knew he hadn't left that pan on the burner. As he ran over to the other side of the kitchen where the stove was located on the far wall, he muttered to himself, "You little shit. You will pay for this." He turned the burner off and reached out for the pan.

The screams could be heard from anywhere in the home. Everybody ran to see what was happening. Those first on the scene just stood back not knowing what to do. The kitchen worker rolled around on the floor writhing in agony, the whole bottom part of his body was covered in scolding oil. A member of staff pushed their way through the onlookers, grabbed a fire blanket off the wall and slipped as he went to cover his body. Even though the hot oil had been on the cold tiles for several minutes, it still burnt his hands when he put them on the ground. He wasn't sure if covering him in the blanket was the right thing to do but he had to do something.

Overcome with pain, the kitchen worker slipped in to unconsciousness, much to everybody's relief. More than half of the residents watching had at one time or another fallen foul to this man's evil ways. Not many of them held much sympathy for him.

As the man was driven off in the ambulance, the home slowly returned to normal, everybody drifted off to discuss their various theories. Fish, who had been one of the first on the scene returned to his bedroom. "Remind me never to mess with you." Leo said nothing as he lay on his bunk facing the wall. He wasn't proud of what he'd done.

Clover House
Chapter 15

The next day Leo visited Julie at the hospital, as he had done every day since the fire. She was able to talk now, though her voice resembled that of a fifty-a-day smoker. He didn't tell her anything about what happened at the home, it was something he'd rather forget.

"They say I can come home tomorrow." Until that moment, Leo hadn't even considered where home would be for Julie. It would have been nice to be together but the homes the others went to looked better. He could forgo her company if it meant she was staying somewhere more friendly. He wondered if where she was going was something she'd considered.

"So where will home be?" he asked.

"Mr Jacobs said he'd organised something. He's picking me up at lunch time tomorrow. I noticed you were limping more than normal. Is your leg alright?"

Leo brushed the subject aside, "It's fine. Will I still be able to come and visit you"?

"Leo you know full well that I wouldn't go anywhere that you're not welcome." He smiled but was still curious where she could be going.

Leo remembered something, "Oh I have a surprise for you."

Clover House

Julie sat up all excited. "I love surprises. What is it?"

"Well I don't actually have it yet. I was watching a TV programme the other day and it reminded me of you," Leo was dying to tell her what it was but had mixed emotions about it. He knew she would love it but it wasn't the kind of gift you just spring on someone.

"What's the point in telling me if I can't have it? That's just teasing." Her bottom lip was out again like a spoilt child.

"I think it will be worth it when you get it," he replied.

As Leo left the hospital he bumped into Mr Jacobs in the car park. "How are you doing Leo? I heard there was a bit of an incident at your new place yesterday."

"It was just an accident in the kitchen, nothing serious." Leo looked down towards the floor so Mr Jacobs couldn't see the guilt in his eyes.

"That's not what I heard. The version given to me was that it was quite serious. It certainly put an end to that young man's career in a kitchen," he waited for a response.

"If you'd tasted the food in that place you wouldn't consider that as such a loss." Mr Jacobs was taken aback by this flippant remark. "Where's Julie

Clover House

going to stay? She told me she can leave the hospital tomorrow."

"She's going to stay with family for a short while. I had a meeting with the builders and the insurance company. They say we should all be able to move back to Clover House in three or four months."

"Family? What family? Julie never mentioned anything about any family. Why can't she stay with them all the time instead of having to live at the home?" Leo said this in a manner that demanded an answer. Mr Jacobs shuffled uncomfortably from one foot to another as he pondered his answer.

"It's not as easy as that Leo. You have to understand that the Julie you have come to know is not the same one as everybody else sees."

"I don't understand." Leo had no idea what Mr Jacobs was trying say.

Leaning towards Leo as though getting ready to pass on a secret, Mr Jacobs put his arm around his shoulder. "Some of what I'm about to tell you is confidential and I would appreciate it if it didn't go any further," Leo nodded hesitantly. Mr Jacobs continued, "Before Julie came to us she had stayed at two Private Care Homes. Unfortunately neither worked out... because of her behavioural problems."

Leo shrugged the arm off his shoulder. "What behavioural problems? Julie doesn't have any

Clover House

'behavioural problems' as you put it." Mr Jacobs took a step back and wondered if he had done the right thing even starting this conversation.

"When she was staying at the other homes, in one she attacked one of the residents and in the second home she violently attacked a member of staff. Remember what she did to Tommy Bishop? Before we got the whole story we all assumed she'd done it a third time." For the next minute no one spoke. Leo was digesting this new information.

"Did she give a reason for attacking them?" Leo just couldn't believe what he was hearing.

"She was questioned by the police but said nothing in her own defence. It turned out that the member of staff that she attacked was on 'The sex offender's list', something that didn't come to light when he was offered the position six months earlier. Now if that had something to do with it we don't know." Mr Jacob continued, "The homes had no alternative but to ask her to leave. That's why she ended up at Clover House, the Council couldn't say no."

Leo was rubbing his fingers through his hair, "And that's why family members wouldn't take her in?" Mr Jacobs said nothing he just nodded his head and agreed. "But that isn't the Julie I know, you have seen her she's the sweetest person you could wish to meet."

Clover House

"I must admit that since coming to Clover House and partnering up with you I had my doubts, I've even read her file several times." Leo looked up at the side of the hospital towards the windows of Julie's ward.

"I don't believe any of this," Leo said before storming away. Mr Jacobs shouted after him but was totally ignored. He shook his head from side to side, locked his car with the remote fob and made his way to the hospital entrance.

"Can I see you in my office Leo?" shouted the Manager of Leo's new home. The request, or order, came as soon as Leo put a foot in the building. Fish was just leaving the office. He didn't make any eye contact with Leo. "Take a seat. I was wondering if you may be able to impart anything further as to what happened in the kitchen?"

"The kitchen?" Leo planted on his face the most, vague expressing he could make.

"Information has come to light that you were seen in the vicinity of the kitchen, not long before the accident." The Manager stared at Leo. After seeing Fish come out of the office Leo wondered if he had said something about his part in the accident. "We have CCTV in the building and the health and safety officer investigating the case thinks there are some questions that need answering."

Clover House

"I'll do whatever I can to help sir," Leo smiled pleasantly.

"Good. Can you tell me what you were doing in the kitchen?" The Manager sat back in his chair waiting for the answer.

"Okay I confess," said Leo. The Manager sat upright so fast he hit his paunch on the side of the desk. "It was me. I went in to steal some food for my roommate. He missed dinner." Leo was taking the gamble that Fish hadn't told them anything. If there was CCTV then it could only have been in the dining room not the kitchen, otherwise they would have seen the kitchen worker abusing the residents. The reason Fish must have been called in as well, is he too would have been seen going in and out of the kitchen earlier.

"Is there anything else I can help you with sir?" Leo stood up to leave. The Manager wasn't happy with Leo's answers but he was limited as to what action he could take.

"Just go Leo." Leo thanked him, wished him good luck with the investigation and left.

Fish was waiting for Leo when he returned to their room. "I didn't tell them anything Leo. Honest." He was panicking that Leo had thought he'd told them about their confrontation with the kitchen worker and they had somehow linked Leo in with the accident.

Clover House

"It's okay Fish. I know you didn't say anything. In fact we'll never mention it again." The Manager had no idea how uncomfortable Leo had felt whilst being questioned. His poker face had paid off. If they could have connected Leo to the accident then he would have been in serious trouble. He just hoped that it would all blow over

Leo decided that he may have been a little unfair to Mr Jacobs when they met outside the hospital. Julie's past wasn't his fault and on reflection he didn't have to tell Leo anything about it, but he had. He would go to the hospital and kill two birds with one stone. Firstly he would apologise to Mr Jacobs and secondly he would see Julie and ask for the address that she would be staying at.

It would be great to have Julie on the outside again. Being so far away from Clover House meant he didn't have the arcade to go to and his recent jaunts around the local area had produced nothing of interest. Leo felt good today. It was the first time he had walked on his leg without pain since the kitchen incident and Miss Bailey, the home's battle axe, had not been into work. As it turned out, she was the Deputy Manager...and the kitchen worker's mother. Yes, everything was good about today.

Clover House

Crossing the hospital car park Leo saw Mr Jacobs's car parked against the side wall, in a disabled parking spot, "Naughty Mr Jacobs." He smiled and promised himself the pleasure of winding him up about it. He walked across the reception and into the waiting lift. As the door closed Leo could have sworn he'd seen the three people who had been visiting Julie the first time he came to the hospital. The problem was they were leaving on their own. When Mr Jacobs had mentioned about Julie staying with family he had presumed that these were the ones. Maybe she's not ready to leave today.

The lift opened and Leo stepped out. He started walking through the ward, saying hello to the other patients in the mini wards. He had come to know a few of them, even helping the nurses out now and again with simple chores.

Arriving at the last one he found a young male nurse making Julie's bed. "Damn have I missed her. Has she gone already?" The nurse stopped what he was doing and looked up. "Cheeky cow, she's left the flowers I bought her. They cost me over ten quid," the nurse said nothing. He just looked at Leo with a blank expression. You could have cut the atmosphere with a knife. A cold chill ran down Leo's back. "Julie Sykes? She has gone home, yes?" Leo was finding it hard to breathe. He looked back through the ward as though he was checking he was at the right one, but he already knew he was.

"Leo, Leo." Recognising Mr Jacobs voice Leo spun around. He looked beyond him hoping to find Julie, dressed with suitcase in her hand ready to go home. She wasn't there. Leo was gasping for breath. He didn't want to hear Mr Jacobs say anymore words. He was scared stiff what they might be. He just stood there eyes glazed over, mumbling a prayer to himself.

Mr Jacobs ran the last few steps and threw his arms around Leo like a long lost brother. "I'm sorry Leo I've been trying to contact you all morning." Leo slowly lifted his face from Mr Jacobs's chest. He looked up at him knowing that he had to hear the words eventually.

"Is she...?" He couldn't finish the sentence.

"No," came the reply he wasn't expecting, but then his hopes were crushed. "Not yet. She had taken a turn for the worse during the night. A combination of the fire, her cancer and all the medication was more than her body could stand. She had a heart attack. The Doctors did everything they could. They managed to revive her but it's just a matter of time." Leo buried his head back into Mr Jacobs's chest and sobbed uncontrollably. He whispered to Leo, "You knew this time would come, you have to be brave for her sake if nothing else.

Clover House

"Where is she now?" he asked, taking the advice and trying to compose himself before seeing her. "Can I go to her, I need to see her." He started straightening his shirt and wiping the tears from his cheeks.

"Of course you can. She's been transferred to another ward. I must warn you first Leo, she looks very ill and there are a lot of tubes and wires. She won't look how you remembered her."

The walk through the hospital corridors took an eternity. They seemed to go up and down stairs several times. It was only when they travelled through a narrow walkway with windows on either side that Leo realised they were moving from building to building. They arrived at ward L18 Jubilee Wing.

During the walk Leo had pulled himself together. His face was no longer red and blotchy. His eyes, though still a little red gave away no trace of how he had taken the news only fifteen minutes earlier. "Are you ready Leo?"

Leo took a deep breath, pasted on his most charming smile and walked straight onto the ward. It didn't hold many patients, but those that it did all looked extremely ill. There were pipes and tubes everywhere. Machines pinged and beeped incessantly. He had to check all their faces twice. It was only on closer inspection that he was able to pick out Julie. Mr Jacobs's warning of how she would look didn't even touch the surface. Like every other patient she was surrounded by machines, tubes disappeared under her bed clothes. Her arms were punctured with needles of every size and description. Julie herself looked like another person entirely. That was until she saw him and smiled.

"No point asking what you've been up to?" said Leo. In these situations he always fell back on his humour to camouflage his real feelings. He tried to look beyond her dark eye sockets and sunken cheeks. How could this be the same person he visited only yesterday? It took all her energy but she raised one hand then dropped it on to the bed as a signal for him to come and sit next to her. He sat down, trying to avoid all the medical equipment. He scooped up her hand and held it gently. He considered putting it to his lips and kissing it, but was scared of pulling out the intravenous drips that seemed to be everywhere.

"Save your energy, don't try to talk." A Doctor appeared from nowhere. He asked who Leo and Mr Jacobs were. They explained how they knew Julie and how they were aware of her previous conditions. When Mr Jacobs introduced Leo as a friend he corrected him by saying, "Boyfriend." Even though Julie's eyes were closed she must have been listening because she squeezed Leo's hand in acknowledgment.

After watching the Doctor checking the equipment and making notes on his clipboard for about fifteen minutes, Leo felt Julie's grip on his hand go limp. He leant forward in a brief panic. "She's gone to sleep, that's all," said the Doctor. "Maybe it's time you gave her a little rest. You can come back in the morning. By then some of the medication should have worn off. She should be more responsive."

Mr Jacobs stood up and tapped Leo's shoulder as a signal to do likewise. They retraced they steps back through the hospital in silence. To try and lift the mood Mr Jacobs joked, "We better find another way to that ward. Or we will need a couple of beds." Looking at Leo's expression you'd have thought he hadn't heard him.

Like snapping out of a trance Leo suddenly turned to Mr Jacobs and said, "I need your help. Actually I need your credit card and a lift, but I'll pay you back." They drove across town to an internet shop Mr Jacobs used to use before he had internet installed in his house. They scrolled through this site and that until Leo found what he was looking for. Mr Jacobs pointed to one of the offers, "That is the cheapest."

Clover House

Leo frowned. "The cost doesn't matter, what matters, is that we can go and pick it up now. Would you also ring the Manager at my home and explain where I am, he'll listen to you."

Mr Jacobs took his mobile out of his pocket. Whilst listing through his contacts he asked Leo, "Are you sure this gift is what she wants, maybe flowers would be more appropriate. Leo didn't think this comment even warranted a reply.

The company's offices were nearly thirty miles away. Entering the building they walked up to the receptionist and gave her their names. "I emailed a Mr Dartford he said if I came to your offices I can collect my order." The receptionist said nothing. She simply smiled and picked up the internal telephone.

"He said he will be be right down. Just take a seat." She then continued doing her nails.

A bald man with a very long beard, and wearing a suit marched up to them. Under his arm he was carrying a small box his other hand was outstretched towards Mr Jacobs, "Mr French I presume?"

"No. I'm Leo French," Leo grabbed the man's hand and shook it.

"My apologies." They all sat down and Leo introduced Mr Jacobs as a friend. Since Dartford's arrival Leo's eyes hadn't left the box he was holding.

Clover House

"We don't normally do business this way, nowadays we do everything over the internet, but given the circumstances allowing you to pick it up was the least we could do." He passed the box to Leo. As he removed each item Mr Dartford explained what it was and its relevance to the complete set. Leo couldn't have been more pleased with the purchase.

Mr Jacobs produced his credit card and offered it to the businessman. "That won't be necessary. I spoke with my boss, who just happens to own the company. When I explained the circumstances and the need for you to collect it straight away, he told me to waive the fee. He lost his daughter in a similar tragedy earlier this year. He sends his regards by the way.

"That's really good of him. Can I thank him personally?" asked Leo.

"Unfortunately not, he's very busy at the moment." Mr Dartford stood up wished them good luck and walked away at a hurried pace, leaving them standing alone. Mr Jacobs started walking the other way towards the exit.

"Just a minute," Leo called after him, he then approached the receptionist. "Can I have the company owner's name? I'd like to send him an email to thank him for something.

Clover House

"Yes, it's Mr Dartford. You were just speaking to him," she returned to brushing her nails once again.

Leo was dropped back off at the home he was staying at. Mr Jacobs agreed to collect him in the morning so they could travel to the hospital together. Entering the room Leo found Fish looking very agitated. "What's wrong?"

"The Manager has had me down in the office again. He's not letting it drop over this kitchen accident," he added the last word of the sentence with a little sarcasm. They keep asking about you and where you were and if you'd ever had a run in with any of the kitchen staff.

"Just forget about it. You weren't there so you don't know anything. It'll blow over." Leo was trying to convince himself as much as Fish. He jumped on to his bed and took the lid off the box he'd just collected. He spent most of that night looking at its contents and staring out of the window.

The next morning when Leo walked out of the building Mr Jacobs was sat waiting for him in his car. Leo opened the passenger door and got in. "You haven't forgotten it then?" Leo looked down at the gift wrapped box on his knee.

Clover House

"No way, I even managed to cadge some wrapping paper from one of the girls whose birthday was yesterday." Mr Jacobs noticed, but didn't want to comment on the choice of wrapping paper, he wondered why it was plastered with the words 'Happy Birthday' all over it.

"I hope the doctor is right about Julie, when he said that she should be more responsive this morning."

"I wouldn't get your hopes up too high Leo. You do realise how ill she is, don't you?" He didn't like to reply to that question. It made it seem final, so he just nodded his head.

Arriving at the hospital Mr Jacobs parked outside the building that housed Julie's ward, rather than having to repeat the trek they made previously. He pulled straight in to one of the disabled spaces. Leo looked at him and lifted his eyebrows. "If anybody's looking just exaggerate your limp," he said, then got out of the car.

Wanting to get there as quickly as possible, Leo was walking at a pace that Mr Jacobs found difficult to keep up with. "Hold on Leo. She's not going anywhere." He regretted saying that as soon as the words left his mouth. Either Leo didn't hear him or he was ignoring him because he didn't slow down. Mr Jacobs caught up with him at the lift.

Clover House

Entering the ward, they could see Julie sat up and talking with the Doctor. She still looked very ill but today there was a little more colour to her cheeks. The Doctor had been right, thank God.

Her face beamed when she saw her two visitors entering the room. "My two favourite men, what more could I ask for." Leo was the first to lean over and kiss her on the cheek he then moved to one side and Mr Jacobs did likewise. The two of them pulled up a couple of chairs and the usual pleasantries were exchanged, 'How are you today? Did you sleep well?' etc, etc.

"What's that?" Julie was looking at the box Leo was holding. "Is it someone's birthday?"

"Let's just pretend it's yours. Do you remember me telling you I had a surprise for you?" he handed her the gift. "Well this is it. I hope you like it." Mr Jacobs shuffled in his chair. He felt a little uncomfortable about what her response might be when she opens it.

Leo had fastened it using too much sticky tape so he had to help her find a starting place so she could begin to unwrap the box. Once she'd started, it didn't take long. She looked up at Leo for a clue before removing the lid. "Just open it." He said.

She looked inside and started taking out the various certificates and maps. "You don't have to wait for the next available one. You have your very

Clover House

own star waiting for you." She lifted the framed certificate from the box. It confirmed that a star had been named in her honour. The new name for the star from now until eternity would be 'JULIE'S PLACE'. "That was what you were going to put on the neon sign, isn't it?" Mr Jacobs had absolutely no idea what they were talking about.

Julie just stared at all the contents from the box spread over her bed. "You do like it, don't you?" Leo held his breath waiting for her to answer.

Julie threw her arms around him, not caring about the intravenous drips that hung from her arms. "It's the best non-birthday present I've ever had." She nestled into his neck. Leo could tell she was crying.

"I think I'll go and get a coffee. Mr Jacobs excused himself and left them alone.

Leo selected the astrological map that pointed the exact position of Julie's star. "I chose a bright one so you can see it clearly. Your window faces west so you don't have to go outside to see it. Of course you will have to wait until it gets dark, and fingers crossed, it's not cloudy" Julie placed the certificate on her bedside table but held the map so she could study it in more depth.

"Will you stay with me until it gets dark so we can see it together?" The odd tear still ran from

Clover House

Julie's eyes. She used a tissue to blow her nose and wiped the tear away so Leo wouldn't see it.

"Of course, I'll tell Mr Jacobs to go home without me and get him to okay it with the home." Right on cue Mr Jacobs re-entered the ward, looking at his watch. "You can go," said Leo as though he was dismissing a servant. "Sorry I mean you don't have to stay, but I would like to if that's okay."

"How will you get back?" Leo hadn't thought of this, the home was on the other side of Leeds so he couldn't walk it and the buses stopped quite early."

Mr Jacobs read his hesitation and pulled out his wallet, "Get a taxi home Leo. There is a taxi rank at the end of the road. I'll ring the Manager at the home and explain," he then dropped a twenty pound note on to the bed.

They were both so grateful.

Waiting for it to go dark seemed to take forever. Fortunately it was a clear night. To fill time Julie asked Leo what he'd been doing. Because nothing much had happened and he didn't want to tell her about the kitchen incident he sat pondering the question for a minute, "Ah I forgot to tell you. Mr Jacobs had a meeting with the builders and it looks like we'll all be back at Clover House in just a few months."

Clover House

"That will be nice for you," said Julie looking a little sad. Leo knew he'd put his foot in it again but tried to salvage the situation by reverting to his humour again.

"What do you mean? I'll be in that shithole while you're on your fantastic star." Julie knew what he was trying to do so she pretended to smile.

Changing the subject Leo pointed out of the window. "Look the first stars are coming out." He grabbed the map and pointed out to Julie the ones he recognised from doing his homework the previous night. "The bright one to the left of those three close together...that's yours."

"Can we call it ours?" another tear appeared.

Leo held her close and whispered into her ear. Of course we can. One day we'll be together for always. They stayed in that position for as long as they could.

The next day there was no rush to get to the hospital because the doctor wanted to do some more tests, so Julie was unable to have any visitors until later in the afternoon. Leo lay on his bed recalling the pleasure Julie had got from his gift. Her face had been a picture. He wished he could give her something else that would produce the same response. Then he had an idea.

He jumped down from his bed and started fishing through some dirty clothes that had just been

Clover House

dumped in the corner of the room, "I'm sure it's around here somewhere." Lifting the last item he found what he was looking for. The camera.

Though his hidden stash of money was still under the floor boards in his bedroom at Clover House, he still had some left over from the Malaga trip in the holdall they'd taken. Lucky for him that had been put in the box with his other belongings. That's where he'd found the camera in the first place. He retrieved the bag and started searching the small pocket inside. He was starting to panic when he found what he was looking for, a small polythene bag containing some notes. He didn't bother counting them he just put the bag into his pocket.

He found a small shop that did digital processing on the parade just several hundred yards from the home. The first thing he needed to buy were some more batteries. He removed the old ones, cursing at the inappropriate time they decided to die on him. He bought some and put them into the camera, hoping nothing had happened to the Malaga shots. It took him a while to find the gallery icon, he selected it. A screen shot of the last images taken was the first on the page, it was a video. Leo pushed play. It showed his face looking into the camera. The background was the kitchen at the home. The camera was lifted up high, this must be when he put it on top of the fridge. A slight

Clover House

adjustment brought the whole kitchen area into focus.

Leo didn't know if he hoped it had captured the beating he received, if it did then what he did to the kitchen worker was for nothing, he had the evidence all along. Even if it did, what could he do with it now? No beating was worth what he did to that man. He watched as the playback showed the man entering the kitchen...then it stopped. It showed nothing else of what happened that day. Leo pushed the delete button.

On the screen was a photo of Julie lying on the sand. The next one was similar only her pose had changed. There were a few of him that she had insisted on taking and some of the surrounding views. This is just what he wanted. He passed the camera to the shop assistant and pointed out the ones he wanted printing. Whilst waiting he went across to the wall that displayed an array of photo frames. He chose the one he thought Julie would like the best, collected his pictures and paid for everything.

Back at the home he was placing the chosen photo into the frame whilst explaining to Fish where it had been taken. Fish couldn't believe he'd had the audacity and the knowhow to disappear to Malaga, just for the day. There was a knock at the door and

Clover House

the Manager's voice shouted out, "Leo, are you in there?" They looked at each other and Leo, leaving everything where it was, jumped up and hid behind the door. He put his finger to his lips in a gesture to Fish to say nothing.

Fish gave it a second and opened the door just a crack, the Manager pushed it a little further open, pinning Leo behind it. "Have you seen Leo French?" He looked beyond Fish and saw the picture and frame on the small desk.

"No sir, not since breakfast. He's probably gone to visit his girlfriend in hospital," The Manager tutted and left.

"Thanks Fish." Leo finished wrapping the frame, slipped it into his rucksack and sneaked out of the home using a rear door.

At the hospital Leo was excited about giving Julie the picture. He could just hear her saying something about having two none-birthdays. He'd already prepared his reply by pointing out the fact that the queen has two birthdays a year. He smiled to himself as he entered the ward.

Suddenly someone grabbed his shoulder, he spun around to see Mr Jacobs looking like he'd been crying, "Hi, Mr..... what's wrong?" Without waiting for an answer he turned and saw that Julie's bed was empty. He looked back at Mr Jacobs.

Clover House

"I tried to contact you Leo. The Manager said you weren't in your room. That you had probably already set off to come to the hospital.

"Where is she? Has she not returned from her tests yet?" He so wanted this to be the case but deep down inside he knew what Mr Jacobs's reply was going to be, he just didn't want to hear it. To postpone the inevitable he just kept talking, "I can pop back later. Or even give it a miss today if she's tired. Can you tell her I'll call back first thing in the morning?" Still not wanting to hear the truth he started walking out of the ward.

"Leo, Leo please come back." He stopped but waited for Mr Jacobs to come to him. He turned slowly. "She's gone Leo." Anybody watching the conversation would have thought an invisible fist had struck Leo in the stomach. He doubled over then crumpled to the floor. A nearby nurse came to give assistance but Mr Jacobs shook his head and she retreated. He went down on to his haunches resting his head against Leo's. "It happened when she was having the tests, another heart attack. She didn't feel anything." Leo was silent but the tears rolled down his face without stopping. "We knew she didn't have long." He felt like he was talking just for the sake of it, Leo wasn't listening to anything he was saying.

Clover House

The drive back to Leo's home was taken in complete silence. The Manager was waiting for Leo and helped him up the stairs and into his room. He tried to take the rucksack from Leo's shoulders but he gripped it with all his strength, so he gave up. Like a zombie Leo climbed up on to his bunk, brought his knees up to his chest and just laid there. The Manager gave Fish a look that said 'Keep an eye on him' before leaving them on their own.

He must have kept dropping off to sleep because sometimes he'd open his eyes and Fish would be there, another time he'd open them and he would be alone.

He heard the door opening so turned and faced the wall. Fish entered and slammed the door behind him. Leo listened as Fish mumbled to himself, he seemed distressed. "Oh God they have it in for you Leo. The Manager has just had me in the office again." Leo wasn't interested in anything anymore. He had completely switched himself off. The mumbling continued...,"It was my fault...You can't take the blame for me...He had it coming...You've been through enough..." Leo slipped back off to sleep. "...I'll tell them that it was me."

Clover House
Chapter 16

The funeral was exactly one week to the day after Julie had passed away. Leo had been told before that the dead normally have to wait at least two weeks so was surprised when Mr Jacobs had rang him with a date. He'd asked if he could see her before the service so a visit to the undertakers had been arranged.

He wanted to do this alone so after agreeing a time and getting the address Leo made the short journey on foot. He was welcomed by a young lady in a black suit that showed him through to a private room, that inside looked just like a small chapel. She escorted him to the coffin lying under a large stained glass window, the top was open. "Take as long as you like," she said before leaving him alone.

Leo had never seen a dead body before, except on television. He hesitated before stepping forward. He took a deep breath and looked inside. Julie had never looked more beautiful. They must have used a photograph because she was wearing her odd earrings, just like when he first met her at Clover House, the dangling one on her left ear and the pearl on her right. Her St Christopher necklace had been positioned so it sat in the hollow of her neck. The blue tint to her hair looked new as well, exactly the same as that first day. The only difference was, that

Clover House

instead of the 'Living Zombies t-shirt she was wearing a white blouse and black trousers. "Bet you wouldn't have chosen those," he smiled.

There was no sign of the dark eyes and sullen cheeks that he'd last seen in hospital. There was even a slight smile to one side of her lips, the one she'd wear when hiding a secret or not wanting to admit something. He bent forward and gently kissed her forehead and said, "We didn't know each other for long, but I think you'll agree, we made the most of our time together."

He left without telling anybody, the young girl stepped out of her office hearing the outside door close.

On the morning of the funeral Mr Jacobs came to the home to collect Leo. He waited for him in the Manager's office. When Leo eventually turned up he was almost unrecognisable. His hair had been freshly cut. He was wearing a new black suit, shirt and tie, along with a pair of brand new shinny shoes. Both the Manager and Mr Jacobs looked at him as though they didn't recognise him. "What? Come on we're going to be late," said Leo and walked back out of the office.

Traffic was quite light this morning and the early cloud cover had dispersed to leave a bright autumn sun that reflected on the wet roads. Some

Clover House

people may have said it was a sign when the 'Living Zombies' came on the radio singing the song that the lead singer had sang to Julie. Mr Jacobs reached for the off button but Leo put his hand over it, so it was left on. "You've missed the turning," said Leo as he looked over his shoulder at the turn off to the crematorium where his mother's funeral had taken place.

"It's not being held there. It's at St Peter's in Horsforth." This was news to Leo. He hadn't asked where the service was going to be held as he had just assumed it would be at the nearest place.

When they arrived Mr Jacobs turned the car into the entrance that was flanked by two large wrought iron gates. "We must be early. The people from the previous funeral are still here," said Leo. The car park was full to busting. A couple of cars were coming out, presumably because they couldn't find a space. Mr Jacobs circled the car park twice but to no avail. He too had to leave and look for a space on the cul-de-sac that ran adjacent to the church.

After finding a parking space and that hadn't been easy, they retraced their steps back to the church. "Why is it being held here?"

"Family choice I presume," answered Mr Jacobs, straining his neck to look up at the massive spire.

Clover House

"That would be the famous, invisible family she had," Leo said sarcastically

"Not today Leo, please."

"I'm sorry, your right. Today is Julie's day."

As they approached the church Leo was amazed to see that everybody was entering and not leaving it. "These people are going in, so they can't be from the service before. Are you sure you've got the right place?"

"I'm sure. Maybe Julie was more popular than you thought," replied Mr Jacobs.

"I thought there was just going to be half a dozen of us, at most." As they approached the church they saw the vicar welcoming people at the entrance. Mr Jacobs was in front so he shook his hand and walked in. It was a few seconds before Leo caught up. "I just had to have a word with the vicar." Mr Jacobs looked at him suspiciously but said nothing.

The church held over two hundred people but already it was becoming difficult to find a vacant pew. Fortunately they were able to squeeze on to the end of one about half way down the aisle. Leo kept looking around at all the people. He still wasn't convinced they were in the right place. If it hadn't been for the conversation he'd had with the vicar he

Clover House

would have demanded that Mr Jacobs make a phone call and double check.

Right at the front sat an elderly lady in a wheel chair. She looked just like Julie, the same features, only older. This had to be her mother, the similarity was uncanny.

"Are you okay? Asked Mr Jacobs

"I'm fine considering. I don't believe what you told me about Julie, I still think she was a good person." Leo started playing with the order of service that had been given to him as they'd entered.

"Of course she was a good person. You don't think a bad person would have this many people attending do you?" This made Leo feel a little better. "And I'm sure her life was made better by meeting you Leo," then he added, "Even though you did give me a merry chase."

Leo put down the piece of folded card and looked at Mr Jacobs. "What do you mean gave you a merry chase?"

"Leo it's like I told you before I have a responsibility for all the residents under my care."

"What does that mean?" He had a feeling Mr Jacobs knew more than he was letting on. He turned to face him and braced himself for the answer.

"Okay let's go back to the police car from Manchester that suddenly appeared outside Clover House," Leo started to flush. "Your description was given in connection with it but I said nothing, though it did make me start watching you more closely. Then I get a phone call from the bank saying someone matching your description is trying to draw money out of an account where I am, what is called the 'Permanent Agent'. That is legal jargon for someone who is given the responsibility for a bank account that is owned by someone like you that is in care. I authorised the money you requested but kept an eye on you. Then I find a sheet of paper you left on the printer showing air ticket prices to Malaga. You can imagine how that made me panic. By the way you had us all running scared when Julie collapsed in the airport shop."

"How the hell do you know about that?" Leo was gobsmacked.

"I had Mr Green follow you out there. He was on the same plane. In fact he said he panicked when the person sat next to him turned around and started telling you how he buys his drinks in the airport rather than pay the airlines prices." Leo could remember the man speaking to him after he complained rather loudly about the price of water. He never guessed that Mr Green was sat next to him.

Mr Jacobs continued, "I had to report back to Julie's family. Like I said it was my responsibility, but they knew she didn't have long. If it hadn't have been the heart attack it would have been the cancer.

Clover House

They told me to do what I had to do to make her last months as pleasant as possible. I thought you were good for her," then he added, "and her for you."

As the last people entered and settled down, unfortunately some had to stand at the back, the organ started playing. The woman sat to Leo's right pulled out a handkerchief and sniffled into it. He had no idea if she was family or friend.

People started looking back to the door so Leo did likewise. As Julie's coffin entered being carried by six pallbearers everybody stood up. Leo wished he could have been one of the pallbearers but nobody had even thought to ask him. The coffin past within inches of his shoulder, he couldn't believe Julie was inside, the box seemed so small.

The service started and the sermon was punctuated with hymns. As it continued more people became upset. Leo had shed every tear in his body over the last week and now consoled himself with the fact that Julie was now in a better place and free of pain.

Towards the end of the service the vicar thanked the choir for their rendition of 'Going home'. He then made an announcement. "One of our congregation has asked if he may read out a poem he has written especially for Julie. Leo French." He stretched out his arm in Leo's direction.

Clover House

As Leo stood up Mr Jacobs grabbed his jacket sleeve. "What are you doing Leo?"

"I'm going to read my poem." Leo stepped out into the aisle and made his way to the front. Mr Jacobs was cringing. He could have accepted this if there had only been a handful of people, but he knew Leo wasn't the brightest of people and was worried that he may embarrass himself in front of everybody.

The vicar stepped to one side and allowed Leo to take his position behind the lectern. "This poem is for the sweetest person I have ever met." He removed a slip of paper from his trouser pocket, unfolded it and spread it across the sloping surface. He coughed into his hand and began reading out loud...

I wonder if it's possible
To live upon a star
I've been searching for you everywhere,
And maybe that is where you are.

I listen for your breathing
But I don't hear a sound
I guess I chose the wrong place
To lay my blanket down.

Throughout our time together you've been my compass north

Clover House

Giving me direction, telling me go forth.
But you left without a warning, there wasn't any sign
And if I had the power I'd surely turn back time.

I'd share with you the thoughts
That dance around my head
My hopes, my dreams, my love for you
The things that went unsaid.

I wonder if it's possible
To live upon a star
I'm hoping and I'm praying
That that is where you are.

He folded the piece of paper, placed it back into his pocket and started making his way back to his seat. The whole congregation remained silent. It was a full thirty seconds before the vicar had composed himself sufficiently to carry on the service.

As the people followed the coffin out of the building almost everyone at one time or another came over to Leo to either shake his hand or simply squeeze his arm in acknowledgment of the love he obviously had for Julie. Many commented on the poem.

Leo stood next to the coffin as they prepared to load it back into the hearse for the short journey

Clover House

to the other side of the grave yard. He removed his wallet from his jacket pocket and looked inside. To his relief the four leaf clover that Julie treasured so much was still in the little pocket next to his lucky 50p piece. Just when he thought he couldn't cry anymore a single tear ran down his cheek and fell on to the leaves. The dampness intensified the emerald green of the plant. He placed it on the coffin lid where he imagined Julie's heart would be. His tear holding it in place.

After they lowered the coffin into the ground the vicar passed around a silver plate containing soil. When it came to Leo he hesitated not knowing what to do. Mr Jacobs took the lead and Leo copied. As they all threw the soil onto the little wooden box, not one of them disturbed the four leaf clover.

Leo didn't go to the wake. He was invited but politely declined. He didn't go straight home either. He watched from a distance as the grave diggers finished their work and when they left he returned to the spot where Julie's body would forever lay. He didn't speak he just stood there looking at the freshly turned soil for several hours.

The vicar caught sight of him as he walked from the church to the vicarage, but experience told him that at times like this people didn't want any company.

Clover House

Leo had been crouched in front of Julie's grave for so long that his legs had gone numb. He stood up straight and stretched his legs he then stepped closer to the headstone the grave diggers had replaced. Julie's name wasn't the only one engraved on the marble. Looking a little more faded was the name and details of Julie's father. It was then that he realised they were at the very same grave he had visited with Julie. His mind had been so distracted that he hadn't noticed.

He wondered if Julie knew that this would eventually be her final resting place. Maybe that is why she wanted to visit it. He now realised what she had said when she touched the head stone on their previous visit. She hadn't said "God be with you," she'd said, "I'll soon be with you." The fact she was now with her father that she loved so much made him feel a little better.

He looked at the details that had been added about Julie. Like her father it gave her age and date of birth.

Julie Sykes
Aged 64 years
1951-2015

So many years had been taken from her.

Clover House

As Leo walked back to the home night set in. He stopped and looked up into the sky. It took him several minutes to get his bearings but when he did a smile came to his face. Was it his imagination, or was 'Julie's Place' shining a little brighter?

Clover House
Chapter 17

'Just 2 years later'

The alarm clock made Leo open his eyes. He instinctively reached over and hit the button on the top, stopping the beeps instantly. He stretched his arms above his head and looked up. He was slightly confused as the colour of the ceiling didn't look familiar. Then looking to the side he saw a framed photograph on his bedside cabinet. It was of a woman laid pointing at something on a beach. She had hair that looked as though it had undergone a blue rinse but she was mainly in the shadows so features were difficult to make out. He stared at the picture trying to recollect a name. He gave up presuming it must be a relative, maybe an elderly aunt.

He brushed the thought to one side and got out of the bed. He walked over to the small sink in the corner of his room and began shaving.

Having completed only one side of his face he washed off all the remaining shaving foam and dried using the towel hanging next to the mirror. He then dressed, put on his shoes and checked himself in the mirror once more before going down to breakfast.

He passed Miss Stevenson on the stairs who said something about it being bad luck to cross like

Clover House

they had, but he just smiled and continued on his way.

At the bottom of the stairs he saw the tray containing all the flowers for the Poppy Appeal. It seemed to trigger something in his memory. Unfortunately it wasn't the fact that he benefited financially from the Appeal, having had his twenty three year career as a Royal Air Force Pilot cut short during a crash whilst carrying out a training exercise. The injuries he'd sustained to his leg prevented him from ever flying again and he was given an honourable discharge.

"My birthday, I am... 72 years old." It was funny how he could always remember his age. What he hadn't realised was the date was the 10th of November, his birthday was tomorrow.

He selected the best looking poppy and using one of the pins provided he attached it to his jumper. He gave it a slight adjustment so it was sitting upright.

He was about to walk away when he remembered something. He removed his wallet from his trouser pocket and looked inside. He knew you were supposed to put some change in the blue container sporting the roundel but only had a five pound note. Opening the little pocket in the side he found a strange looking 50p piece, so without a

Clover House

second thought he dropped that in and listened as it hit the other coins in the bottom.

"Good morning Leo," said Mr Jacobs. Leo smiled and continued through into the dining room. He shook his head sadly as he watched Leo limp away. Even though he'd been the Manager of Clover House for over twenty years, and was proud that it carried the reputation of being one of the best 'Homes for the Elderly' in Leeds, he still thought it depressing to see the effect that Alzheimer's can have on people.

Leo had been at the home for about eight years. When the first signs of the disease started showing, his mother who was then eighty four, found it very difficult to deal with his frustrations. The illness had progressed at a slower rate than in most people, but the last two years had shown a marked decline. He was no longer allowed to leave the home without a companion, usually a member of staff.

He sat down at the oak table and was just about to pull his chair under when Marge tapped him on the shoulder and pointed at the seat he was supposed to be occupying. Leo changed positions without saying a word.

A bowl of porridge was placed in front of him, so Leo tucked the napkin into the top of his jumper, picked up his spoon and started eating. He looked

Clover House

around the table at faces that looked familiar but he was unable to put a name to a single one of them.

A rather over weight woman with long grey hair sat opposite him. He was sure her name began with an 'M' and for some reason he knew deep down inside that he didn't like her. She was helping to feed breakfast to a fat man that never spoke. Each time she offered him a spoon full of porridge more of it ended up on the table cloth than inside his mouth. He looked at the scar that ran above the man's right ear and wondered if that had anything to do with his limited ability to speak and feed himself. "Come on Tommy, open your mouth wider," said the woman trying to shovel another spoon full into his half opened mouth.

Hearing that name triggered the memory of another name from Leo's past. He looked up and down the table then grabbed the sleeve of the woman from the kitchen who was placing a plate of toast on the table. "Where's Fish?" asked Leo.

She smiled kindly and said, "he's still in the secure unit Leo. Do you remember he did something very, very, bad?"

Leo smiled back, "who did?"

Leo wasn't feeling very hungry. In fact he wasn't feeling very well at all this morning. He put down his cutlery, stood up and walked over to the door. He looked over his shoulder at the woman

Clover House

from the kitchen then at everybody around the table. He then turned and walked through the hall and up the stairs. He paused for a few seconds looking at the doors along the corridor then opened the nearest one.

"Your room is next door," said the man lying on the bed. Was it his imagination or was everybody talking to him like he was a child? He opened the next door along the corridor and felt a little relief when he recognised some of his personal possessions.

Even though Leo had only been up for less than two hours, he changed into his pyjamas and got into bed. He lay looking at the ceiling trying to guess what colour it should be, "blue," he said finally. "That ceiling used to be blue." As he said this he felt the side of his mouth slip to one side, his vision in one eye became blurred and he could feel pins and needles down his arm. Not an unpleasant feeling he thought.

He lay like this for some time. His pillow was starting to feel damp from the drool coming out of his mouth. He struggled to turn his head to one side then he mumbled some words and forced out a twisted smile. Though the words were undecipherable, what he actually said was...

"Julie. I'm coming home."

The End.

Clover House

Author's note

The idea for this story came about fourteen years ago when a family barbeque was brought to an abrupt end by the British weather. I was sat on a bench with my mother, who was then sixty-six years old. "I could just go dancing," she said half to herself and half to me. I asked her to repeat what she'd said.

"You heard me," she replied.

The discussion then continued with her telling me her theory about aging. She said that by the age of twenty, virtually all your future opinions, likes and dislikes will have been made, and that is the age that you stay mentally for the rest of your life. "Just because I sit here while everyone runs around getting my food and drinks doesn't mean that this is where I want to be. At this precise moment I would like to be out dancing."

I tried to test her theory by bringing up objections but each and every one she shot down without hesitation. "You don't think a seventy year old man looks at a seventy year old woman do you? No he looks at the girls he would have looked at when he was twenty. And has your taste in music or food changed much since you were twenty? I think

Clover House

not," she said before I had a chance to agree with her.

As I came around to her way of thinking I tried to put myself in her shoes. I asked, "Is there anything that you wish you could have done but never got around to it?"

Without hesitation she said, "I wish I had learnt how to swim."

The following week I took her to the local swimming baths several times until she finally got the hang of it. She could now swim. The only problem was that she didn't like getting splashed by all the youngsters that were using the pool at the same time. So she joined a private gymnasium with its own swimming pool.

One day she was stood outside the fitness area watching everyone exercise on the machines when one of the young instructors walked passed and invited her in. "I couldn't possibly, I wouldn't know what to do." The young man persuaded her to go in and he spent the next forty-five minutes setting up and showing her how to use each machine.

My mother at sixty-six had caught the fitness bug. She now arrived at the gym at 6am every morning and did one hour in the fitness room before going through to the swimming pool for another hour. Inevitably if you saw her anywhere she would be wearing a tracksuit and 'Nike' trainers.

Clover House

She continued this regime for the next four years until unfortunately my father past away. This really hit her hard. She didn't go to the gym as much and we also realised that she was starting to repeat herself and forget things.

A year later and it was obvious there was something wrong so we took her to the Doctors, who after a number of tests confirmed that she had the early signs of Alzheimer's disease.

Fortunately the progression was quite slow and her attitude was optimistic. If anyone ever asked her how she was coping she would often reply. "It's not such a bad thing; at least I don't have any worries because I can't remember them." If anybody started speaking to her like a child or asked her a stupid question, which happens more often than you would imagine, then her stock reply is, "I'm called Lily, not silly!"

Ten years on and as expected her memory has deteriorated. On a recent visit to us in Spain she would appear each evening with her suitcase in hand asking if it was time to leave as she didn't want to miss her train back to London. She currently lives in Leeds and hasn't been back to London (where she was born) since she was fourteen.

When she told me her theory on aging all those years ago, I understood that although your opinions, likes and dislikes stick from the age of twenty, you still gained memories after, that enrich your life. Alzheimer's disease gradually eats away at your short term memory taking you right back to being a child again, and like a child my mother has to be reminded to carry out simple tasks like cleaning her teeth and changing her clothes.

    I sometimes think instead of calling the disease Alzheimer after the discoverer Alois Alzheimer back in 1906, it should have been called 'Benjamin Button Syndrome', after the film where Brad Pitt is born an old man and as he increases in age he becomes younger.

    I'm guessing that because you couldn't see the characters in this book you inevitably presumed that they were young. That is because in their minds they were.

For Lily Cuthbertson   -   Forever young.

Also by

Alan Cuthbertson

Fiestas and Siestas Miles Apart

Fiestas and Siestas Miles Apart is the humorous but true story of what happens when the Cuthbertson family decides to sell everything (including the family business), load the family car, and move from England to Spain.

As author Alan Cuthbertson and wife, Heather, begin their move, daughters Ashlie and Stacey have other ideas and take off on their own adventure to Thailand, Australia, and New Zealand. The girls swim with sharks and work in a gold mine, their enthusiasm and naivety shown in the emails and texts received by their parents, who themselves are finding Spanish life a very steep learning curve. Who knew fried sparrow was a delicacy? And Alan's first hunting trip is not a completely successful expedition, but a very funny one.

Clover House

Eventually the Cuthbertson family finds the house and village of their dreams, but this is just the beginning of their adventures in Spain…

Excerpt from
Fiestas and Siestas Miles Apart

Antonio and Encarna are good friends from our village. Antonio is referred to as Lee Van Cleef, getting the nickname after I pointed out his similarity to the spaghetti western star

****

A couple of days later we sat with Van Cleef and his wife Encarna and the conversation got onto the subject of food once again. "Rabbit is my favourite," confessed Van Cleef.

"I've never had rabbit," admitted Heather.

"*Mi casa, Domingo próximo*." Van Cleef's invitation to Sunday dinner will have been the first time we have eaten with a proper Spanish family in their own home. It was something we looked forward to with mixed emotions.

Not knowing Spanish etiquette for such an occasion, we dressed casually and before leaving the house, selected a bottle of wine to take. "I've just remembered. Encarna doesn't drink and Van Cleef only drinks whiskey," said Heather, so I swapped the bottle of wine for one of whiskey.

Clover House

During the short walk to their house, Heather and I mulled over the possible menu.

"He said it was going to be rabbit," I pointed out.

"I'm just thinking back to the bar when they were all eating sparrows and snails," Heather said nervously, her nose curling a little.

"We have to eat whatever they put in front of us," I said, "it would be rude not to."

We knocked on the door and were greeted by Van Cleef himself. I passed him the bottle of whiskey. He looked at me, then the bottle, then back at me. His expression said, "You have a drink problem my friend." Inside the house it was quite dark, as most Spanish houses are. Alfonso, Van Cleef's son, was engrossed in a cartoon on the TV and seemed to be finding it hysterical, a little unusual when you consider he is 19 years old.

We took our positions at the table and right on cue in walked Encarna carrying individual plates full of assorted vegetables and…some kind of animal. Heather and I glanced at each other recalling our vow to eat, or at least try, whatever was put in front of us.

Now I know this was to be Heather's first taste of rabbit but I just don't ever remember seeing a rabbit with wings, so presumably some kind of last minute substitution had been made. We all picked up our knives and forks and began to dig in. Encarna saw me pushing the meat around, got up and disappeared in to the kitchen. When she returned she passed me a pair of scissors. "What the hell are

Clover House

these for?" I whispered to Heather. Across the table from me, Alfonso had rejected the knife and fork and was pulling the animal on his plate apart with his fingers, so I did likewise. The wing looked tempting so I gave it a tug. It came away from the body. Unfortunately where it had been joined hung the veins and tendons, still dripping with blood and bodily fluids.

"*Antonio, no conejo*?" Not rabbit? I asked.

"*No*," he replied. He then stood up, hooked his thumbs under his armpits and waved his elbows up and down. From this I deduced he was either trying to tell me we were eating bird, or we had progressed on to charades and this was his Dick Van Dyke in *Mary Poppins*.

Heather, who had been sitting at the side of me throughout the meal, let out a faint squeal that fortunately only I heard. As I turned my head I saw her pulling something from her mouth. Was it a bone? A bit of gristle maybe? Or even a filling? No, it was a piece of buck shot the size of a small rock. "I guess he shot it himself," I said.

After the main course, a bowl of fruit was brought from the kitchen, and Heather selected a pear and took her first bite. "*No, No*," called Encarna thrusting a knife toward Heather.

"I think she wanted the pear," I said a little worried. As it transpires, the knife was to peel the pear, as they never eat the skins of fruits concerned about what they may have been sprayed with.

As we said our goodbyes I returned the invitation and promised that next time they would

Clover House

have to come to our house for a meal. Van Cleef turned his nose up and curled his top lip. A rough translation of what he said would be. "I don't think so; I don't eat that English muck."

Made in the USA
Charleston, SC
18 November 2015